DETROIT PUBLIC LIBRARY

W9-ADQ-131

AR BL4.4

DENIM DIARIES 5:

RAISING KANE

Please Return To
Parkman Branch Library
1766 Oakman
Detroit, MI 48238   MAI 13

PA

DENIM DIARIES 5:
RAISING KANE

DARRIEN LEE

www.urbanbooks.com

Urban Books, LLC
78 East Industry Court
Deer Park, NY 11729

Denim Diaries 5: Raising Kane Copyright © 2010 Darrien Lee

All rights reserved. No part of this book may be reproduced in any form or by any means without prior consent of the Publisher, except brief quotes used in reviews.

ISBN 13: 978-1-60162-233-4
ISBN 10: 1-60162-233-3

First Printing December 2010
Printed in the United States of America

10 9 8 7 6 5 4 3

This is a work of fiction. Any references or similarities to actual events, real people, living, or dead, or to real locales are intended to give the novel a sense of reality. Any similarity in other names, characters, places, and incidents is entirely coincidental.

Distributed by Kensington Publishing Corp.
Submit Wholesale Orders to:
Kensington Publishing Corp.
C/O Penguin Group (USA) Inc.
Attention: Order Processing
405 Murray Hill Parkway
East Rutherford, NJ 07073-2316
Phone: 1-800-526-0275
Fax: 1-800-227-9604

DENIM DIARIES 5:

RAISING KANE

Prologue

Denim nearly rear-ended the car in front of her but was able to swerve into a McDonald's parking lot and bring her car to stop. She screamed as she struggled to get her seatbelt off, but before she could get out of her car, a hand reached up from the backseat and grabbed her arm.

"Stop screaming before somebody calls the cops!"

With tears streaming down her face, Denim looked into her rearview mirror and saw the panic-stricken face of a young girl.

"Who are you? And why the hell are you hiding in my backseat?"

The young girl started sobbing as Denim's heart started to slow down to its natural rhythm.

"I'm sorry. I didn't mean to scare you," she

replied through her sobs. "My name is Kane. I live right behind you on the next street."

"That doesn't explain why you're hiding in my car."

"It's personal. I just need to get away."

Denim studied the young girl for a moment and then said, "Get out of the backseat, Kane. I can't talk to you like this."

Denim watched the girl climb out of the car. Dressed in a pink-and-green future AKA T-shirt, denim jacket, and green pajama pants, she appeared to be around Denim's age, but Denim wasn't sure.

"What's going on so bad that you feel like you have to run away?"

"I said it was personal. Look, don't worry about me. I can find my way from here."

Concerned about the teen, Denim decided to push her for more information. She wouldn't be able to live with herself if she let her go and something bad happened to her.

"Are you hungry?" Denim asked.

Kane looked toward the McDonald's. "Not really, but I wouldn't mind one of those mocha coffees."

Denim retrieved her purse and cell phone out of the car and said, "Then let's go. My treat."

"I can't go in there dressed like this."

"You look fine. All teenagers dress like that."

Kane walked with Denim into McDonald's and waited as she ordered two bacon, egg and cheese biscuits and two mocha coffees. They took a seat in a booth near the play area.

Before they could start talking, a woman walked over to them and grabbed Kane by the collar of her jacket, knocking her coffee out of her hand. As she yanked her out of her seat, she slapped her across the cheek and yelled, "What the hell are you doing here? I thought I told you to get me some money! Get in the goddamn car!"

Chapter One

The woman pulled Kane down the aisle and toward the door, angrily cursing at her.

Denim was stunned. She was so shocked, she couldn't move as Kane called out for help. *Do something, Denim,* the soft voice said in her ear, but she couldn't. She was frozen with fear, not knowing who the woman was, or if she had a weapon.

But she had to do something. So she prayed that she could somehow find the strength to help save the young girl. Then, as if jolted with a surge of power and courage, she slowly stood and ran full speed toward them. She felt like she was dreaming, no longer in control of her body or movements. How in the world did she end up here, in a battle for the life of a stranger? But she wasn't just any stranger, she was a girl, approximately her

age. She could be anyone . . . her or even her friend
Patrice begging for someone to come to her aid.

Denim jumped on the woman's back to try and
knock her down so Kane could get free, but the
woman quickly turned her body around and was
able to push Denim on the floor. Hard.

"I don't know who you are, but this has nothing
to do with you!" She screamed at her.

By that time the manager of McDonald's walked
over and prevented the woman from dragging
Kane out of the store.

"Get out of my way, bro!" she yelled. "Don't
make me cut you. She belongs to me!"

Denim quickly picked up her cell phone and dialed 9-1-1, while the manager of the store continued to block the door, preventing the woman from
taking Kane out of the building. Other patrons in
the restaurant were just as shocked as Denim was
as they watched the altercation play out between
the manager and the unknown woman.

"Help me!" Kane yelled.

"Ma'am, I can't let you leave with this girl," the
manager said to the woman.

"The hell I can't!" She tried to push past him
while still holding Kane by the collar.

Denim made eye contact with Kane and wished

there was more she could do than pray the police would arrive soon.

The manager yelled, "Ma'am!"

The woman swung a knife at him, cutting his shirt but just missing his skin. She kicked the door open and dragged Kane out into the parking lot and threw her into the arms of a large man. He opened the front door of the car and shoved her into the front seat.

Before he could drive off, the police arrived, blocking his vehicle. With guns drawn, they ordered all three of them out of the car and down on the ground.

"I didn't do anything wrong!" the driver yelled as he was instructed to put his hands on his head.

Another officer pulled the woman out of the car and handcuffed her before helping the shaken young woman out of the car. He inspected her for injuries. After not seeing any injuries, he turned his attention back to the woman.

Denim ran out of the McDonald's. "Are you OK?"

Kane nodded, tears flowing out of her eyes.

"You're making a mistake, officer! That's my god-damn daughter!" The deranged woman yelled.

Shocked, Denim looked at Kane and asked, "Is that really your mom?"

Kane nodded, clearly embarrassed.

Denim put her arm around her shoulders to comfort her. She would be embarrassed too if her parents were loud, obnoxious, and obviously drunk or high.

The woman yelled as police officers put her in the backseat of the car. "Kane! It's going to be all right, baby!"

"Young lady, is that your mother?" one officer asked.

"Yes, sir, but she doesn't live with us."

"Where do you live?"

"I live with my father and two younger brothers over on Nichols Street."

"Did she harm you in any way?"

Kane reluctantly pointed to her face and said, "She slapped me, and when that man threw me in the car, I hit my head."

The officer took down the information as well as her personal information. "Give me your father's number so I can call him to come get you, because your mother is going to jail. She's obviously high, and she's going to be charged with assault, not only against you, but the store manager."

"I don't want to press charges, officer. She's my mother, and she's sick," Kane replied nervously.

"You mean she's an addict, right?"

"I just want to go home, officer."

The officer closed his notebook. "I'm sorry, young lady, but you're a minor. I have no choice but to contact your father. The laws are very clear with regards to minor children. I have to notify your father."

Denim could see the distress in Kane's face and felt like she needed to intervene. "Officer, I live across the street from Kane. I can drive her home."

"What is your name?" the officer asked.

"My name is Denim Mitchell. I live at 103 South Jackson Street, which is one street over from Kane."

The officer jotted down the information and then said, "You can take her home, but I'm going to have another officer meet you at the house, so he can talk to you and your father."

"Thank you, officer."

As Kane and Denim walked toward her car, they could hear her mother yelling out, "Kane! I'm sorry, sweetheart. I'll be home soon. Don't worry. I love you!"

Denim could see her friend trembling. "It's going to be OK, Kane. Just get in the car."

Kane quickly got inside the car while Denim started the ignition.

As they drove down the street, Denim looked

over at her passenger and noticed her tears. "Are you sure you're going to be OK?"

Kane nodded and said, "I'm sorry I got you involved in this."

"What exactly did I get involved in?" Denim asked. "Is your mother really an addict?"

Kane turned to Denim. "My mother's been on coke for about a year. My dad was able to get her into rehab twice, but each time she checked herself out before she could get well. Both times he let her come home, thinking he could cure her, but she started stealing things out of the house.

"One day I came home and found my mom and some guy passed out on our sofa. That was the last straw. My dad kicked her out of the house, and we moved to try and get away from her, but as you can see, she found us. She showed up at the house this morning looking for money and food. I still love my mother, so I couldn't turn her down. She's just sick."

"Was your dad at home when your mom came by this morning?"

"He wasn't at first, but he forgot some paperwork and had to come back and get it. When he caught my mom in the house, he went ballistic. They got into a huge argument, so I ran out of the house and hid in your car."

"Don't you think your dad is worried about you?"

She shrugged her shoulders. "Maybe. I know he's pissed that I let my mom in the house because he'd told us under no circumstances should we let her in, but I felt sorry for her."

"What about your brothers? How old are they?"

"Christian is eight years old, and Justin is eleven."

"I see. You know the police will probably be there when you get home.

Are you ready to face your dad?"

"I'm going to have to face him at some point. I might as well get it over with. I'll probably be grounded until I'm twenty-one after this."

"You don't know that. I'm sure your father is really worried about you."

Kane turned to Denim and said, "I hate living like this. Since my mom's been sick, I had to take care of my little brothers, which means I have no life. I don't get to go anywhere or do anything I want to do."

Denim reached over and took Kane's hand into hers and said, "I'm sure your dad will understand. Just tell him how you feel."

"That's easier said than done. My father is very strict."

"My dad is strict too. Just talk to him, Kane. If he sees how unhappy you are, I'm sure he'll come around."

By the time Denim pulled up to Kane's house, they could see her dad standing on the porch talking to a police officer.

"They didn't waste any time getting here, did they?"

"No, they didn't." Kane opened the car door and got out.

Denim rolled the car window down and said, "Kane, keep your head up. And if you want to talk, remember, I live just around the corner."

"Thanks, Denim."

Before pulling away, Denim quickly wrote down her cell phone number and handed it to Kane. "Call me later and let me know how things turned out."

Kane tucked Denim's number inside her jacket pocket and said, "I will. Thanks for everything."

Denim pulled away from the curb and prayed that her neighbor would find a solution to her family issues, besides running away.

Denim was already late to work, so she didn't see any harm in jotting down her thoughts in her diary before entering the building:

I'm late to work, but it's all good. This morning started out very scary. First, I thought I was going to be carjacked, only to find out it was my neighbor hiding out in my backseat. Her name is Kane, and she's about my age. Her mother is an addict, and she assaulted her this morning. I could've gotten hurt trying to help her, but I'm happy to report that we're both OK.

Well, physically at least. Kane has a lot of emotional drama going on at home. I pray things work out for her and her family. In the meantime I gave her my number so she could call if she wants to talk. Now I'd better get to my job before I won't have one.

Smooches,

D

Denim quickly tucked her diary back inside her purse and hurried into the building.

"You're late!" Tony said to her when she walked into the clinic.

"I know, I know, and I'm sorry. I had to help a friend this morning, and it took longer than I expected."

Her boss, Tony, pointed over to a waiting patient

and said, "We'll talk about it later. Mrs. Freeland has been waiting on you for nearly an hour, and she won't work with anyone else but you, so get to it."

"I'm sorry, Tony. I promise I'll make it up to you and stay over if I have to."

He smiled and said, "You're one of my best physical therapists, Denim, and our patients expect us to be here. Don't make this a habit."

"I won't," she replied as she helped Mrs. Freeland up from her chair and took her over to the treadmill to begin their therapy session.

Denim loved working at the physical therapy clinic. She'd started there as part of a work-study program at her high school, but she'd done so well, upon completion of the program, she was hired as a part-time employee.

Kane sat in the family room and waited for her father to finish talking to the police officer. When he entered the room, he looked at her and said, "Kane, I'm so disappointed in you right now. How many times do I have to tell you that you are not to go near your mother? And why in God's name did you let her in this house?"

"I'm sorry, Daddy."

"You always say you're sorry, but you keep enabling her. What are you waiting on? For her to clean us completely out, or for her to let one of her boyfriends in to rape you? Wake up, Kane! Your mother doesn't want to get clean."

Tears fell out of her eyes. "I said I'm sorry, Daddy. Momma said she was hungry and that she needed a little money to get something to eat. She begged me."

"She made her bed, and now she has to lay in it. I refuse to let her bring this family down any farther than she already has. She made her choice, and she chose drugs. I've done all I can to help her. Now she has to help herself."

Kane began to sob out loud as her father yelled at her, but in a matter of minutes, his emotions switched gears. He never could stand to see his only daughter cry, and seeing her now was breaking his heart. He pulled her out of her chair and embraced her.

"Don't cry, sweetheart. I love you. We'll get through this one way or another, but you have to trust that I'm making the right decision about your mother and this family. OK?" He tilted her head upwards and inspected the bruised area on her cheek. He gently caressed her face and said, "Did your mother do this to your face?"

"Yes, sir."

"After all this and you still want to help her?"

"She doesn't know what she's doing when she's high, Daddy. She didn't mean to hurt me."

"How did you get all the way over to Mickey D's? It's four miles from here."

She pointed toward the backyard in the direction of the Mitchell's house and said, "When you and Momma started yelling at each other, I couldn't take it. All I wanted was to get away, so I hid in the backseat of the girl's car who lives in that house. Her name is Denim."

"Why would you get inside a stranger's car? Do you know how dangerous that was? You don't know anything about them. You could've been taken God knows where."

"I know, Daddy. I wasn't thinking. I didn't mean to scare you."

"When I realized you had left the house, I didn't know what to think. I was afraid that you had gone off and gotten yourself hurt or killed. How did you mother find you at McDonald's?"

"I don't know, Daddy. Maybe she was just passing by as I was going inside the restaurant. All I know is that she needs our help."

"I know she does, but I can't do anymore than I already have, and I swear to God, if she ever touches you again, I'm not going to be responsible for my actions. I have a restraining order against her, which means she's not allowed anywhere around you guys, so stop making it easy for her. Think about your brothers, Kane."

She wiped her tears and asked, "What about me, Daddy? All I ever get to do is go to school, cook, clean and take care of my brothers. I don't get to do anything I want to do."

He took her by the hand and sat down next to her. "I'm sorry, Kane. I'm doing all I can to provide for you and your brothers, and to do that, I need your help. We all have to make sacrifices that are not going to be popular, so I need you to work with me. I need you here to help with the house and the boys. Can I count on you until I can find another solution?"

Kane nodded and said, "Yes, sir."

Kane didn't want to disappoint her father. She knew alienating them from their mother was necessary for them to be in a stable environment. For now she would help as much as she could, and pray that either her mother got well or her father could hire a nanny to help with the boys in order to free up her time so she could be a normal teenager.

Chapter Two

Downtown at the central precinct Kane's mother, Yolanda Alexander, was booked and thrown in a holding cell, where she would slowly come down off her high. She'd been a regular visitor over the past year, so officers knew her by name. Her companion, known on the streets as Popcorn, was also thrown in jail with more serious charges of possession of a controlled substance with intent to distribute, and a firearm.

Yolanda lay down on the hard, metal bench of the cell and began to shiver. She needed a fix bad and would do anything to get high.

One of the four other women occupying the cell decided to approach her. "Hey, bitch! You're in my spot. Get your ass up and move it on the other side of the room."

"Leave me alone," Yolanda said back to the woman.

"What did you say to me?" the woman asked.

Yolanda rose up from the bench. "I said leave me the hell alone and take your big ass over on the other side, because I'm not moving."

Before Yolanda could lay back down, the woman grabbed her by the hair and pulled her off the bench and down on the floor. Yolanda got up swinging and cursing. She was about four inches shorter and fifty pounds lighter than the woman, but she held her own as they fought each other for the prime spot on the bench.

The other women in the cell began cheering as Yolanda got the woman in a headlock and started punching her in the face.

The guards finally entered the cell and separated them.

"Break it up, you two!" one officer yelled. "Alexander! You have a visitor! Stop before I send you up to the county jail."

Yolanda turned the woman loose. "Who's here to see me?"

"I don't know!" the officer yelled at her. "Just move your ass!"

Yolanda smoothed down her hair as she followed the officer down the corridor and up a series of stairs until they entered the visitor's area. She was shocked to find her husband waiting on the other side of the glass, and by the look on his face, she knew it wasn't going to be a pleasant visit.

She sat down and picked up the telephone, and he did the same.

"What are you doing here?" Yolanda asked with an irritated tone.

"I came to try and talk some sense into you. You've made a fool of yourself once again. Are you ready to go to rehab and stay this time?"

Yolanda wiped her nose with her hand. "Rehab doesn't work for me."

"You haven't given it a chance. Can't you see what you're doing to your children? You're killing them, Yolanda, along with yourself. You can beat this if you try."

She pounded the table with her fist. "Don't come down here and try to use my children against me. I love my kids!"

"The only thing you love is the high. The children are just an accessory to you."

"Whatever!" Yolanda yelled through the telephone. "I don't have time for this."

"Are you going to go to rehab or not? Think hard, Yolanda, because this is the last time I'm going to try and help you."

She lowered her head. "I can't go, Myron. I'll die in rehab."

"No, you're going to die on the streets, if you don't change."

There was an awkward silence between them for several seconds before Myron spoke up and said, "If that's your final answer, then this is good-bye. You're on your own now. I have the restraining order against you, so you know you're not allowed anywhere near me or the children."

"You can't keep me away from my children!" she yelled.

"Yolanda! I could have you locked up for good for putting your hands on Kane. If you touch her again, I'll kill you myself."

"I wouldn't have hit her if she had just given me the money," Yolanda yelled.

Myron put his hand up to her and repeated slowly to make sure she understood where he was coming from. "Yolanda! I'm serious, if you touch my daughter again, I'll squeeze the life out of you. Stay away from Kane and the boys. You've lost your rights to them."

"Go to hell, Myron! You don't love me. You never did. All you wanted was someone to warm your bed and give you babies. I'm not stupid!"

Myron laughed. It was obvious that Yolanda was still high because, if she remembered correctly, he used to worship the ground she walked on. They'd met in college and both had budding careers after graduation. Myron worked in insurance, and Yolanda was a successful real estate agent to the wealthy. They were making a lot of money and had a beautiful home, but when she started hanging out with some of her wealthy clients, she got hooked on cocaine and lost her job, her livelihood, and her family. Their comfortable lifestyle went downhill, causing them to give up their beautiful home, but Myron was able to bounce back and get the children back into private school.

"Is this the last memory you want your children to have of you? In jail, high, and sleeping around with every Tom, Dick, and Harry you meet?"

"My children know I love them!" she screamed at him.

"And they love you too. That's the sad part about this whole thing. You're trying to make me out to be the bad guy by not letting you come home, but my children's safety and well-being come first, and

I can't let you traumatize them any farther. It's over, Yolanda. I'm filing for a divorce." Myron hung up the telephone and stood to leave.

Yolanda jumped out of her seat and started pounding on the glass. "You bastard! I'll get you for this! You can't take my kids from me!" She screamed through the glass. "Don't you walk out on me!"

Myron calmly turned to his wife. "You gave your children away the moment you became a slave to drugs. Good-bye, Yolanda."

Myron's statement made her angrier. The police officer had to pull Yolanda out of the room kicking and screaming.

When Myron made it back to his car, he leaned against the steering wheel and sobbed. "These are the last tears I'll ever shed for you, Yolanda," he said to himself before turning on the ignition and driving off.

At the Alexander home, Kane's brothers sat on the floor of her room asking her questions about their mother. Since their mother left, Christian had been the hardest hit. He was the baby and was a momma's boy, but Kane had tried her best to step in and comfort him the best way she could.

"Why does Momma love drugs more than us?"

"Drugs confuse people's minds. They don't think straight, and it affects their emotions as well. Momma's not the mother we knew a year ago."

Christian stood and walked over to the window. "Parents always tell kids to say no to drugs. Why did Momma do it?"

Kane sighed and joined her brother at the window. She could hear the pain in his voice as he spoke. She put her arm around his shoulders. "Momma was working long hours, entertaining clients. I think she got caught up with the wrong crowd, li'l brother. Not all addicts look like the crack addicts you see on TV."

"But I miss her, Kane. I want her to come home."

"I want her to come home too, but she can't, as long as she's on drugs."

"Is Momma going to die?" Justin asked. "I read online where most drug addicts end up dying from disease, organ failure, and overdoses."

Kane walked over to him. "I don't know. We're going to have to pray real hard for Momma because Daddy's done all he can do for her."

The mood in the room had gone from sad to depressing. Kane realized she needed to do something to uplift her brothers' spirits.

"Who wants pizza?" she asked.

Christian stood and walked toward the hallway. "I'm not hungry."

"Christian! Wait! Don't leave!" Kane called out to him.

"Let him go, Kane," Justin said. "He'll come around in a little while."

Kane's heart ached for Christian, but she had to give him his space.

"What about you, big brother? Are you going to eat a little pizza with me?"

He looked into his sister's eyes. "I'm not hungry either, but I would like to play a little Uno, if you're up to getting beat."

Kane smiled and said, "Bring it on."

The sister and brother went downstairs to the family room and pulled the deck of cards off the shelf. Before they could deal the first hand, their father walked through the front door, surprising them.

Kane made eye contact with her dad and could see the stress in his eyes. "What's wrong, Daddy? I thought you went to work."

Myron sat down on the sofa. "After the morning we had, I felt like I needed to work from home today. Where's Christian?"

"He's probably in his room crying," Justin said. "He misses Momma."

"We all miss your mother, Justin, but she can't be here in the condition she's in. So, right now, all we have is each other. It's going to be tough, but we can get through this if we stick together."

"What about Momma?" Justin asked.

Myron put his hands over his face in despair. "I'm sorry, son. Your mother's not in the equation right now. My main concern is you, your brother, and your sister, period."

Justin looked over at Kane and started dealing the cards in silence.

"I'm going upstairs to check on Justin, and then I'll be in my office. If you guys want to talk, I'm here."

Justin and Kane watched as their father slowly climbed the stairs. Their mother's addiction had clearly taken a toll on him physically and emotionally. He seemed sad all the time and hardly ever laughed anymore. Considering their mother was his college sweetheart and the love of his life, it was understandable.

"Justin, we're going to have to help Daddy. I love Momma, but look what she's done to him."

"The only way we can help Daddy is by helping Momma first. She has to go to rehab. If she don't, we're going to lose him too. Can't you tell he's lost weight?"

Kane nodded. She thought about her neighbor, Denim. More than ever, she needed a friend and was hoping Denim was up for the job. She had her cell number and thought about calling her but she didn't want to be a pest. She'd call her later, after giving her brother a good spanking in Uno.

Upstairs, Myron found his youngest lying across the bed, staring at a picture of his mother. "May I come in?" he asked.

Christian rolled over and wiped the tears from his face.

Myron sat on the side of the bed and took the picture out of his hand and smiled. "She's beautiful, isn't she?"

Christian nodded. "She looks just like a princess."

"She sure does. Listen, son, I know this situation with your mother is hard on you. You know I would never keep your mother from you guys if she wasn't a risk."

Christian shrugged his shoulders, not clearly understanding what his father was trying to tell him.

"Christian, do you understand why your mother's not here?"

"You said she was sick on drugs."

"She is, and with prayer and luck, your mother

will one day see that she needs to be in a hospital. Until then, I want you to know that I love you, and I plan to make life for you guys as safe, pain-free, and comfortable as I possibly can, with or without your mother. OK?"

Christian hugged his father's neck. "OK, Dad. I love you too."

Myron patted Christian on the head. "Why don't you go downstairs and play cards with your brother and sister? I'm going to do a little work in the office. Later, we'll go out to dinner."

Feeling much better, Christian smiled and made his way downstairs with his siblings.

Myron made his way into his office and closed the door. Physically spent, he practically collapsed in his chair. Sitting there in silence allowed him a moment to recap the chaotic morning with Yolanda and the children. He remembered happier times and he craved happiness again. In the meantime, he had to do what he needed for the sake of his children.

Myron picked up the telephone and dialed his attorney.

Within seconds, he answered, "Anthony McKinney speaking. How may I help you?"

"Mr. McKinney, it's Myron Alexander. I need your help again."

"Myron, it's so good to hear from you. How are the children?"

Myron smiled. "The children are fine. Thanks for asking. We did have a situation this morning."

"What happened?"

"Yolanda showed up at the house after I had left for work. She wanted Kane to give her money. Thank God I forgot some paperwork and had to come back home."

"Myron, she's in violation of the restraining order."

"I know, but my children were so upset about me kicking their mother out of the house."

"Listen, Myron, you said yourself that you felt like your wife was a danger to your children. You put the restraining order in place for a reason. Next time one of them could get hurt, or worse."

"I know, Mr. McKinney, and I appreciate everything you've done for me and my family. But I need to know what my options are, if I wanted to have Yolanda hospitalized."

"Most rehab clinics are strictly voluntary. If you can prove she's a danger to herself or others, you might get her admitted to a mental institution, where she could get the rehab she needs."

"I don't want her life completely ruined by having her committed."

"Are you under the impression she's not ruining her life on the drugs? Myron, it's your decision, but it's my experience that most drug addicts don't stop unless they want to, or are forced to. Which road do you feel like your wife is on?"

Myron thought to himself for a moment. "I get your point. Yolanda got arrested for assaulting Kane and a manager at McDonald's."

"Your daughter, Kane?"

"Yes."

"That's my point. Is Kane OK?"

"Kane's fine, and the funny thing is, she still loves and wants to help her mother. We can't keep going in circles, so I want you to also look into helping me file for divorce. I can only help Yolanda if she wants to help herself, and she refuses, so I have to move on with my children."

Mr. McKinney sighed. "Myron, I know this is difficult for you, and believe me when I say I hate seeing any marriage or family break up, but you're doing the right thing."

"I hope so."

"Myron, this is outside the realm of attorney-client relationship, but I look at you as more than just a client. You're a friend too. And you're going to have to keep your head up for your children's sake. Your mood will set the tone for their mood. If you're down, they'll be down, and if you're happy, they'll be happy. I know it's a tough job, but somebody has to do it."

Myron smiled. "You're right, and I appreciate your honesty, advice, and friendship. I have to do what's best for my children. Thank you. And let me know what I have to do to get the divorce proceedings started. I can't do this anymore."

"Let me handle that. You concentrate on your children. I'll be in touch."

"Thank you, Mr. McKinney."

"It's *Anthony*, and you're welcome. I'll be in touch."

Myron hung up the telephone and decided to join his children for a few hands of Uno before beginning work.

Chapter Three

Denim kicked off her shoes and sat down on the side of her bed. It had been a long day at the clinic. Now all she wanted was a hot shower and some of her mother's delicious meatloaf.

Just before she could get in the shower, her cell phone rang.

"Hello, babe. What's up?"

"Thinking about you," Dre' replied. "Are you just getting in from work?"

"Yes, and I am worn out. We had a full house today. What are you doing?"

"Finishing up a painting for church. I was hoping you would want to go out, but it sounds like you're beat."

Denim smiled. "I'm never too tired for you, Dre'. What do you have in mind?"

"First of all, is it going to be cool with your parents?"

"What are you talking about? My parents love you."

Dre' laughed. "Please! Your pops either gives me the eye, or a pep talk, every time I leave the house with you. He's not dumb. He knows my intentions."

Blushing, Denim said, "Daddy also knows how much I love you."

"Uh-huh. Anyway, I thought we'd go over to The Vibe."

The Vibe was a local teen spot with arcade-style games, great food, and the latest music.

"Sounds like fun. Give me about thirty minutes to get ready and I'm all yours."

"I like the sound of that. See you soon, babe."

Denim hung up and made her way downstairs to clear the date with her parents. They allowed her to date Dre' with particular guidelines and prior permission.

"Mom, Dad, is it OK if I go over to The Vibe with Dre' for a few hours?"

Denim's father put his newspaper down and said, "I thought you were so tired."

She blushed. "Daddy—"

"I'm just repeating what you said when you got home. Now you're all energized. What a miraculous recovery!" he joked.

Her mother smiled and said, "Denim, I don't have a problem with you going out with Dre` just remember our rules and be home by eleven."

Denim kissed her mother on the cheek. "Thank you, Momma."

"What about me? Don't I get a thank you?"

She slowly made her way over to her father and wrapped her arms around his neck. "I'm sorry, Daddy. Thank you too."

Denim hurried upstairs into the shower so she could get ready for her date. After flat-ironing her hair, she slid into a pair of her favorite skinny jeans, an Aéropostale T-shirt and hoodie, and a pair of boots. Before leaving her room, she sprayed a little of her favorite scent, Victoria's Secret Amber Romance, on her wrist and neck before making her way downstairs to wait on her date.

To her surprise, he had already arrived. "Dre'! How long have you been here?" She gave him a hug.

He kissed her on the cheek. "Not long. You smell nice."

"Thank you."

Dre' took Denim by the hand and walked toward the door. He was so handsome in his baggy jeans and sky-blue button-down Sean John shirt. Dre' always dressed in the latest styles, and they fit his six-foot-plus frame perfectly.

"Good-bye, Daddy! Good-bye, Momma!"

Samuel Mitchell walked the young couple to the door. "You two, buckle up. And, Dre', make sure you drive carefully."

"I will, sir."

Samuel watched as Dre' opened the car door for his daughter. She was growing up so fast, he realized she wasn't his little girl anymore. She was budding into a beautiful young woman, and he knew it was only a matter of time before he would be dropping her off at college and walking her down the aisle at her wedding. Until then, he would cherish every hug, kiss, and moment he had left with her.

Dre' backed the car out of the driveway and quickly headed down the street. At the four-way stop sign he leaned over and gave Denim a sensual kiss on the lips.

"What was that for?" she asked with a smile.

After he pulled through the stop sign, he said,

"You know I can't go more than a few hours without kissing you, and I couldn't kiss you like I wanted to in front of your dad."

"Yes, you can."

He glanced over at her and said, "No, I can't, because when I kiss you, I have to feel all of you, and I don't think your father would appreciate where I put my hands."

Denim giggled and put her hand on his thigh. "You have a point, and just for the record, I can't go more than a few hours without kissing you too."

Dre' smiled. "You keep that up we won't make it to The Vibe."

Denim folded her arms. "And the problem is?"

"Denim, you don't need to tease me right now. My parents aren't home, and I have no problem making a detour."

Denim reached over and took him by the hand. She said softly, "Maybe we can go by your house after we leave The Vibe."

He looked into her eyes. "Are you sure?"

She leaned over and gave him a kiss on the lips. "More than anything. I love you, Dre'."

"I love you too."

Dre' continued to drive across town toward their destination. His heart was so full of affection for Denim. She'd been his first and only love, and if everything went as planned, she would also be his wife, after college of course. He also had big plans of going to the NBA and opening his own art gallery. The young couple had charted their future and they were very careful with the choices they made. They didn't want any obstacles to steer them from their goals.

As the couple chatted about school, their friends, and their families, they were interrupted by Denim's cell phone. She pulled her cell phone out of her purse and answered it.

"Hello?"

"Is this Denim?"

"Yes. Who is this?"

"It's Kane Alexander. We met this morning."

"Hi, Kane. How are you?"

Kane smiled and said, "I'm much better than I was this morning."

"Good. I really hope things work out for you."

"Thanks for all your help. Look, if you're not busy, I would love it if you would come over to meet my dad and my brothers. We're ordering pizza."

"That's so sweet of you, Kane, but I'm out with my boyfriend right now."

"I'm sorry, Denim, I didn't mean to disturb you. I'll let you go."

"You're not disturbing me. How about this? I'll give you a call after church tomorrow. We can hang out then, if it's OK with you."

"I'd like that," Kane replied.

"Cool. I'll shoot you a text tomorrow."

"OK. Have a nice time with your boyfriend."

"Oh, don't worry. I will," she replied in a mischievous tone. "Good-bye, Kane."

"Good-bye, Denim."

Just as Denim hung up her cell, Dre' pulled into the parking lot of The Vibe. "Who is Kane?" he asked, as he put the car in park. "I hope it's not a dude you were talking about hooking up with tomorrow."

"Calm down, Dre'. Kane is a girl. She's my new neighbor."

Dre' pulled the keys out of the ignition. "You've never mentioned her before."

Denim lowered her head. "I just met her this morning. Can we talk about this later?"

Dre' could always tell when Denim was hiding something, and today was no different. He trusted her and was just joking about Kane being a guy. Denim had a history of getting in complicated situations, and her demeanor indicated something was definitely going on.

"Are you ready to be straight with me? I know

something's going on, so you might as well tell me."

Denim looked over at him. "Don't be mad."

Dre's jaw tensed up. Anytime she started their conversation with that, he knew he was going to be angry. "Stop stalling, Denim, and tell me what's up with this Kane chick."

She took a deep breath and began to tell Dre' how she met her new neighbor early that morning. As she told the story, she could see Dre's eyes getting red, and the vein in his neck pulsating. He was clenching his jaw so tight, his face looked like stone.

When she finished the story, he looked over at her and asked, "What is it with you? Do you have a death wish or something?"

"I knew you would be pissed. That's why I wanted to talk about it later."

"Why?" he asked angrily. "Did you think I would feel any different than I do now? Babe! You have got to stop sticking your nose in other people's business. Damn! Don't you realize you could've been killed?"

"I wasn't thinking about my safety at the time," Denim said, tears falling out of her eyes. "All I was thinking was, I had to do something to help Kane. I wouldn't have been able to live with myself if she had gotten killed and I didn't do anything to help her."

Dre' climbed out of the car and walked around to the passenger side of the vehicle. He opened Denim's door and pulled her out of the car and into his arms. As he held her tightly he asked, "Don't you know I wouldn't be able to live with myself if something had happened to you? Stop taking chances like that. That's what the police get paid to do."

Denim looked up and saw the weary look in his eyes. "I'm sorry, babe. I hate seeing you freaked out like this over me."

Dre' put his finger on her lips. "Promise me—No more heroics. You're not Superwoman. I have plans for us, which means, marriage, children, and growing old together. Stop trying to mess it up. Understand?"

Denim cupped his face and gave him a slow, sizzling kiss that ignited both of their bodies.

"I understand, Dre', and I promise not to worry you anymore. I want to grow old with you too."

"Cool. Now let's go have some fun," he said as he took her by the hand and started walking toward the door of The Vibe. "I need to shake these images I have of you getting hurt out of my mind."

Before walking inside, Denim stopped him and said, "I really am sorry, Dre'."

He smiled and patted her on the backside and with a sly grin replied, "I know you are. I'll let you make it up to me later."

The young couple made their way inside the building filled with bright lights, loud music, and the smell of pizza, burgers, and chili cheese fries. They met up with a few friends from school, which made the night even more fun.

Before long, Dre' had forgotten all about Kane. He noticed Denim yawning and checked the time. It was going on nine o'clock and he wanted their evening to wind down with her in his arms. He walked over to her as she was chatting with some girls on her cheerleading squad. After speaking to the girls, he wrapped his arms around Denim's waist and asked, "Are you ready to go, babe?"

"I'm ready whenever you are," she answered before saying good-bye to her squad members.

As they walked arm in arm across the room, Denim said, "This was fun. I'm glad I came."

Dre' took one more sip of his soda. "Me too—except for all the guys that tried to hit on you."

"They weren't all hitting on me, Dre'," Denim answered as she re-applied her lipstick. "Most of the guys here know we're together. Besides, you were the one who had your female fan club following you around all night."

Dre' smiled. She was right. He had drawn just as much attention from the opposite sex, if not more. "I guess we're both guilty, huh?" he joked.

Denim linked her arm with his and started walking toward the exit. "You might be guilty, but I'm innocent. These guys don't have a chance with me, so you don't have anything to worry about."

As they stood in line to exit, Dre' planted one last heated kiss on her lips to reaffirm their relationship to anyone present who questioned its stability. "I only have eyes for you too, boo."

Denim smiled and cuddled with her lover. It was time for some private time, and both of them were looking forward to a romantic nightcap to their wonderful evening.

"Where are we going now?" Denim asked as they climbed into his car.

"To my house," he answered as he put the car in reverse.

Denim's heart was starting to pound in her chest. Whenever they got together, it was physically and emotionally intense, and usually left her breathless and in tears.

"Where are your parents?"

Dre' smiled. "Where are they most Saturday nights?"

"At the casino?"

"Exactly, and they won't be home until tomorrow."

Denim bit down on her lower lip. This meant they would have free rein of his house, no interruptions or distractions, just the two of them loving each other, heart to heart, soul to soul, skin to skin.

Later, Dre' dropped Denim off at home and walked her to the door with only fifteen minutes to spare. She was exhausted and overflowing with love and joy for the man in her life.

"Good night, babe," he said softly to her before kissing her tenderly on the lips. "I love you."

"I love you too, Dre'," she replied as she held onto his waist, not wanting to let him go. "Drive safely, and call me when you get home."

Dre' kissed her once more before releasing her. "I will, thanks to you. Sweet dreams."

Denim couldn't help but smile as she climbed the stairs to her room. It was a perfect ending to a perfect night. But she wasn't going to sleep until she knew Dre' was safe and sound at home. It would take him about fifteen minutes to get home, so she had time for a quick shower before receiving his call, and they talked until nearly midnight.

Before going to bed, she made another notation in her diary:

It's almost midnight, and I'm laying here feeling like I want to scream Dre's name from the mountaintop. Well, actually I did that a couple of hours ago. LOL! I spent the evening with him, and without giving away any details, let's just say that he knows how to make me happy. The way he looks at me, touches me, kisses me, and ... well, you know. He's my soul mate for life.

Smooches!

D

Chapter Four

Yolanda picked up her personal effects at the front desk. She was happy to be getting out of jail, but she didn't expect to see the familiar face waiting for her in the lobby. Her makeup was smeared, and her hair was in disarray, so she smoothed down her hair to try and make herself presentable. The jeans and the Grambling University hoodie she had on were dirty, and she needed a shower bad.

"I didn't expect to see you here. How did you know I got locked up?"

Leon was her boyfriend and enabler of her drug addiction. He put his arms around her shoulders and led her outside. "You know word travels fast. Did you get the stuff?"

"I tried, Leon, but my kids—"

He pushed her away and yelled, "I thought you said it would be a piece of cake?"

She opened the car door. "It would've been, if Myron hadn't come back home and caught me and threw me out of the house."

Leon paused before getting inside the car. Once inside he said, "You owe me five thousand dollars, Yolanda, and I want my money. So you either get the jewelry, or I'll go get it for you. You've been living it up with my merchandise, but now it's time to pay up. You can't keep living off me free of charge. I've taken good care of you, and now it's time to pay up."

Yolanda looked at him in disbelief. She hadn't lived with him free. In fact she'd paid her way two times over as his live-in maid. He'd also used her as a marketing tool for his growing "pharmaceutical business," passing her around to prospective clients. Riding on what little high she had left now, she was angry. But she wasn't ready to bite the hand that fed her just yet. If he felt like she owed him, he was mistaken, and it seemed like she would have to show him quicker than she could tell him. In the meantime, she would try to get her jewelry, but to do that, she would have to try and appeal to Kane once again. This time, though, she would approach her differently and try to be sober when she did.

"Are you going to get the jewelry or not?" Leon asked, interrupting her thoughts.

"Have you forgotten that my husband put a restraining order on me? I could go to jail. He could've had me locked up tonight, but he spared me because of our children."

Leon was listening to Yolanda, and she wasn't the Yolanda he normally had control over. He reached inside the glove box and tossed a small package into her lap. "That's enough talk about your kids. Are you ready to party?"

Yolanda picked up the small packet and stared at it. She was feeling bad and could use a little boost, but she really wasn't feeling it tonight. After lying in the jail for hours, all she wanted right now was a hot shower and some clean clothes.

She slid the small packet into his pocket. "Not tonight, Leon. I'm tired and just want to go to bed."

"Do you know how much money I spent getting you out of jail tonight? I want to party, and I want my woman to party with me." He tossed the packet back into her lap. "Now go ahead and get yourself fixed up. You'll feel better, especially after you change into that pretty black dress I bought you last week."

Tears filled Yolanda's eyes as she opened the packet and inhaled the evil substance. She closed her eyes. Her head felt as if she was on a roller-coaster going at warp speed. It was going to be another long night indulging in forbidden fruit. A night that wouldn't end until the morning sun rose on a new day.

Denim exited the church with her parents and made her way through the crowd to chat with her best friend Patrice, who was holding her infant son, Alejandro.

"Pastor was off the chain today, wasn't he?" Patrice asked as she propped her son on her shoulder.

"He sure was." Denim caressed Alejandro's small back. "Patrice, he's getting so big. What are you feeding him? Steroids?"

Patrice giggled. "Everything! Denim, my baby can eat! Seriously, he's eating some table food, because that baby food just isn't doing it for him."

"Let me hold him."

Denim loved holding her godson. He was so handsome with his caramel skin tone and wavy black hair. Alejandro looked into Denim's eyes and smiled, warming her heart.

"Patrice, he is so cute. You can't help but want to hold and kiss him all the time."

Patrice wrapped one of her braids around her fingertip, one of her nervous tics. "Thanks, Denim. But Alejandro is starting to act like his daddy. He can be very demanding when he wants something."

"Stop lying on this baby."

"I'm not lying. You know how loud he cries when I don't get his bottle to him fast enough."

Denim kissed his chubby cheeks. "Don't listen to your momma. You're a sweet little angel, Alejandro."

"Whatever!"

"Patrice, you've lost some more weight. You're smaller than you were before you got pregnant. Are you working out?"

Patrice twirled around in her form-fitting teal dress. "I'm trying," she said. "I think I'm ten pounds lighter than my original weight. That's why I want to go shopping. I need some more clothes. And I need some girl time. You've been working so much lately, I hardly ever see you anymore."

"I'm sorry, Patrice. You know I'm still working, and I have a lot going on at school."

"Dre'—Don't forget to add him to your list," Patrice joked.

With a huge smile on her face Denim said, "I don't get to see Dre' as much as I want to."

"Sure, you don't. DeMario said all Dre' talks about is you. I think he loves you more than basketball now. He's in love with you, Denim."

"I love him too, Patrice. I honestly can't see myself with any other guy. He's so sweet and amazing."

"When was the last time you guys hung out?"

Denim blushed. "Last night."

"Last night, huh?"

"Yes, Patrice, last night. Is there anything else you want to know?"

Patrice studied her best friend's body language and facial expression. She smiled. "You know what? I do have a few more questions, but since we're standing in front of the house of the Lord and you have that goofy smile on your face, I'll save my questions for the mall. Remember, I know you, and I know big-head Dre'. You and Dre' are on fast-forward. Are you sure you two are going to wait until you get out of college before you get married? Because I don't think he's going to be able to wait."

Denim noticed her parents walking in their direction and whispered, "I'll tell you later."

The Mitchells approached the two and greeted Patrice before announcing to Denim they were ready to leave.

Denim handed Alejandro back to his mother. "I'll call you when I get home to let you know what time I'll pick you up. Is Alejandro going to the mall with us?"

"If he's awake, I'll take him."

"OK. Tell your parents I'll see them later."

"I will. You know they're always the last ones leaving. Daddy has to help count the money."

Denim laughed and rejoined her parents at the car. They all climbed inside, and Samuel pulled out of the church parking lot. On the ride home Denim noticed that her father kept glancing at her through the rearview mirror.

"Did you have a good time last night?" he finally asked.

"Yes, sir."

"Where did you guys go?" Valessa asked.

The questioning got Denim's undivided attention. She sat up in her seat. "I told you, Mom, we went to The Vibe. What's with all the questions?"

"Don't get sassy, Denim. We're just making conversation, and we're only asking because somebody said they thought they saw you and Dre' at his house."

Denim stopped breathing. Is it possible that her parents knew about her rendezvous with Dre'? Just in case, she decided to tell the truth. "It's possible. We went by there for a little while before he brought me home. Did I do something wrong?" she asked, trying to feel her parents out.

"You tell me," Samuel responded. "How long were you guys at his house?"

"I don't know, Daddy. Not long. We were just hanging out."

Valessa turned to Denim. "Sweetheart, we're just concerned. We know how close you are with Dre', and we just want to make sure you make good decisions. One mistake can affect you for the rest of your life."

There it was. It was finally out there, so Denim responded the best way she knew how.

"I'm not going to get pregnant, if that's what you guys are hinting at. The last thing I want to do is disappoint you, which means I want to finish college before I start having kids."

Samuel was so engulfed in the conversation, he

had to slam on his brakes to keep from rear-ending the vehicle in front of him.

Valessa looked over at her husband. "Samuel, keep your eyes on the road and try not to kill us before we get home."

"Sorry."

Valessa turned back to her daughter. "Denim, we're only having this conversation because we love you and only want the best for you. Dre' is a nice young man, but please don't let your feelings for him cloud your judgment."

"Mom, neither my head or heart is clouded, and neither is Dre's."

Valessa smiled. "Sweetheart, just remember that I told you Dre' will not be the only love in your lifetime."

Denim turned her head, so her parents wouldn't see her, and rolled her eyes. There was no way she would ever love another guy the way she loved Dre'. Now all she wanted to do was change the subject. "If you say so, Momma."

Valessa glanced over at Samuel. "By the way, you cut it pretty close to your curfew last night."

Frustrated, Denim challenged her parents in a way she hadn't in a long time. "Why are you riding me so hard about Dre'? Did I do something wrong by going over to his house? I thought when you let me start dating you were going to let me date. Am I not allowed at his house now?"

Samuel pulled the car into the garage and shut the engine off. He climbed out of the car and opened the door for his daughter. As she climbed out of the car, he pulled her into his arms and said, "Denim, we love and trust you, but if we feel like you're dating recklessly, we can and will shut it down as quickly as it got started. Therefore, if we have questions or concerns about where you're going with Dre', don't get defensive, just answer our questions. I'm all for being reasonable, which means I'm all for a reasonable discussion on any subject. OK?"

"OK, Daddy. And I'm sorry if you felt like I was challenging you guys."

"Apology accepted."

Denim turned to her mother and said, "Mom, is it OK if I go to the mall later with Patrice? I haven't had a chance to hang out with her for a while."

"That's fine, Denim," Valessa said, unlocking the door. "Tell Patrice's parents I said hello."

When they walked into the house, they were

greeted by Denim's brother, Antoine, a law student in D.C.

"Antoine!" Denim screamed and jumped in her brother's arms. She hadn't seen him in a few months and was so excited that he was home.

"Hey, sis! What's cracking?" Antoine hugged and kissed Denim.

"Why didn't you tell us you were coming, son?" Samuel asked.

Antoine sat his sister in his chair. "I wanted to surprise you." He hugged and kissed his parents.

"How long will you be home?" Valessa asked.

"A week," he replied, massaging his sister's shoulders. "Now, what's for dinner, Mom? Because I'm starving."

"You're always starving." Valessa sat her purse on the countertop. "I have a roast in the oven. You'll be able to eat in about an hour, but if you're really starving, there's some leftover lasagna in the refrigerator."

"That's OK, Mom. I'm going to take Denim out for brunch." Antoine pulled Denim out of her chair. "We'll eat dinner later."

"Can't I change first?"

Antoine picked up the car keys. "Yes, but hurry up."

Denim sprinted up the stairs to change into some jeans. She was so happy that her brother was home and couldn't wait to spend some quality time with him. Before rushing back downstairs to join him, she pulled out her diary and wrote:

Oh my God! Antoine is home! I've missed him so much. Got to go!
Smooches!
D

Chapter Five

Kane looked out the window toward Denim's house. She washed the dishes left over from breakfast, while her brothers played the Wii game in the family room.

Myron, her father, walked into the kitchen and picked up the dishtowel and said, "Do you mind if I help?"

"No, I don't mind, Daddy."

He smiled. "You know I appreciate everything that you do around here. You're my angel, and I couldn't do it without you."

As Kane washed the skillet, she said, "I know, Daddy, and I love taking care of the boys. It's just that sometimes I . . ."

"I know, sweetheart. I still need to let you be a teenager, and I want to apologize for putting so many demands on you."

Kane handed the skillet to her father. "Thanks, Daddy."

Myron turned on the radio while they cleaned the kitchen, and within seconds one of his favorite songs came on. He grabbed his daughter by the hand and started dancing with her. She giggled as he twirled her around.

Justin and Christian heard all the commotion and ran into the kitchen to see what was going on. Upon entering they saw their father and sister dancing to a Charlie Wilson song, so they immediately started dancing as well.

They were a happy family most of the time, despite the void, and did their best to make the most of a bad situation.

Once the song ended, Myron hugged his kids. "You guys, go get dressed so we can go out."

"Where are we going?" Justin asked.

"You kids need some new clothes, so I thought we would check out that new outlet mall a few blocks over. You're growing out of everything."

Justin and Christian ran for the stairs, but Kane stayed behind to talk to her father.

"Dad, I'm glad you're smiling again."

He hugged her and said, "Me too. We still have a tough road ahead of us, but we'll get through it. Now go get dressed so we can get out of here."

Kane and her father made their way upstairs together so they could get dressed, and an hour later they all climbed into Myron's BMW X5 SUV and pulled out of the garage.

At the mall Kane and her family made their way from one store to the next. Her brothers were particularly anxious to get to the City Gear store because they'd had their eyes on some shoes and jeans. Next door to City Gear was a Charlotte Russe store.

"Daddy, is it OK for me to go in here while you take the boys into City Gear?" Kane asked.

"Sure, sweetheart, and take your time."

Denim turned to enter the store and nearly knocked a patron down. "I'm so sorry," she said. "Are you hurt?"

"Kane?"

"Denim?"

Denim smiled and said, "What a nice surprise! How have you been?"

Embarrassed, Kane nodded and said, "I'm good. How about you?"

Denim linked her arm with Antoine and said, "I'm great."

"Is this your boyfriend?" Kane asked.

Denim burst out laughing. "I'm sorry, Kane. This is my brother, Antoine. Antoine, this is Kane. She lives in the house behind ours."

Antoine shook Kane's hand. "It's nice to meet you. Look, I'm going to let you two chat while I go over here and look at some jewelry."

Kane watched Antoine as he walked away. "He's cute, Denim. How old is he?"

"Too old for you," she replied with a smile. "Kane, my brother is twenty-four years old, and he has a girlfriend."

Kane pulled her purse up on her shoulders. "You can't hate me for asking."

They walked over to some chairs and sat down so they could talk.

"Are you here by yourself?" Denim asked.

Kane pointed toward City Gear and said, "No, I'm here with my dad and brothers."

"Great! I'll get to meet them." Denim turned their conversation to Kane's mother. "Have you heard from your mom?"

The smile immediately left Kane's face. She looked into Denim's eyes and said, "No, I haven't. My dad took out an order of protection against her, so she can't come around us anymore."

Denim took Kane's hand into hers. "I'm sorry,

Kane. Look, I didn't mean to dampen the mood. I'm happy I ran into you."

Kane stood and said, "Me too."

"Listen, me and my friend Patrice are going to the mall later. Are we still on?"

"Sure," Kane replied with excitement. "Come on so you can meet my family."

Denim followed Kane into City Gear, where she was introduced to Myron and the boys. After a short chat and receiving her dad's permission to go shopping, Kane waved good-bye to Denim.

As Denim made her way down the hallway to the jewelry store to rejoin her brother, she caught him flirting with a sales lady. She decided to put him on blast. "Hey, bro! What are you doing? Looking for an engagement ring for your girl, Danielle?"

"No," he answered as he slowly turned toward his sister and gave her the eye. "Have you finished socializing so we can get something to eat?"

"Yes," she answered as they walked out of the jewelry store.

"By the way, she's a cute chick," Antoine pointed out. "How long has she been our neighbor?"

Denim pulled him by the arm. "Not long, and she's jailbait, so don't even think about it."

Antoine looked at his watch and laughed. "I figured that. Come on so we can get something to eat. Aren't you supposed to meet Patrice?"

"We're meeting later. Right now all I want to do is hang out with you."

They entered the food court together and began to scan the various choices.

"So, what's up with you and Dre'? Is the honeymoon over yet?"

Denim playfully punched her brother in the arm. "Dre' is perfect, and no, the honeymoon is not over. In fact, it's only just begun. He's so sweet, Antoine. I love him so much."

"I've heard it all before, sis. Do you want a gyro?"

Denim nodded and continued to talk about Dre'. Antoine listened to his sister talk about the love of her life while he placed their order for two gyros, salads, and drinks.

Once they were seated, Antoine took a sip of his soda. He said, "I don't want to talk about Dre' anymore because I don't like to think about you and him like that. How's school? And your job at the clinic?"

"School's good; I'm still on the honor roll. And I'm making a lot of bank from my job."

Antoine laughed. "That's good to know. Now I can stop sending you money."

"No, you don't," she answered with a laugh.

Antoine often sent his sister money and gifts. He loved spoiling her. "I figured you would say that. What are you doing with all that money you're making?"

"I'm saving some of it, but I do my share of shopping too. Didn't you notice my new boots?"

He looked down at her feet. "Nice!"

What Antoine didn't know was, she was also saving up to get him a new set of Nike golf clubs. Presently, he was playing with a used set he'd found at a pawnshop, but she wanted him to have his own. In a few more weeks she was going to finally have enough to purchase it, and she couldn't wait.

"While you're all up in my business, what's going on with you and Danielle?"

"Danielle's fine as always. She asks about you all the time."

"We stay in touch over Facebook." She held her gyro up to her mouth. "I like her. You need a strong woman like her to keep you in check."

"No, what I need is my little sister to stop growing up so fast."

She wiped her mouth with a napkin. "Well, that's not going to happen. I'll be out of high school in another year, and then it's on to bigger and better things."

"The bigger and better things is college, right?"

"Something like that." Denim winked at him.

Antoine leaned back in his chair. "Don't play with me, li'l girl. What are you up to?"

"I'm not up to anything," she answered with a slight grin. "All I'm saying is, college is in my plans, but there might be something else a little more important ahead of it."

"What's more important than college?"

Denim winked at her brother and decided to have a little fun.

Then, as if a light bulb went off, Antoine's mood went from joyous to concern. "You have got to be kidding me. Surely, you're not thinking about doing what I think you're thinking about."

"If anybody understood I thought you would. You know what it feels like to be in love."

"If you're talking about getting married, you've lost your damn mind. You can't get married, Denim. You're too young."

She smiled. "But we love each other."

Antoine was angry now. He pointed his finger at his sister. "You and Dre' are thinking with your hormones and not your brain. You're going to college, and you're going to graduate, period. You can do what you want to after that."

She stared at him and then said, "We'll be eighteen, which means no one can stop us. Not our parents and not even you, big brother."

"I think you've forgotten who I am, sis." Antoine laughed.

"No, I know exactly who you are and what you're capable of, but we're getting married a few months after we graduate. Our minds are made up."

"Then what? How are you going to support yourselves?"

"We'll manage. Dre' makes good money selling his art, and I have money saved up."

Antoine stood and silently started packing up his food.

"Where are you going?"

"You made me lose my appetite. Let's go."

"Come on, Antoine," Denim pleaded with him. "I need you in my corner on this one."

Antoine started to walk off, but then he turned back to her. "Denim, if you think I can't stop you from making the biggest mistake of your life, you have another think coming."

Denim could see her brother was ready to explode. She couldn't help but burst out laughing.

"What's so damn funny?" He asked angrily.

"Big brother, you just got punked!"

Antoine pushed his chair up to the table. "That bullshit wasn't funny, Denim."

Pleased with her performance, Denim hugged his neck and said, "Admit it, bro—I got you."

Antoine tried to remove her arms from around his neck. His heart was pounding in his chest. She had gotten his blood pressure up, and he realized he needed to calm down. "Yeah, you got me, all right, but I'm not convinced you were really joking."

"It was a joke. We're not planning a wedding."

Antoine shook his head in disbelief. "Nah, I wouldn't put it past you and Dre' to actually try and pull a stunt like that. I know how tight you guys are."

Denim laughed even harder before wrapping her arms around his waist. "It was a joke, Antoine. I didn't know you were going to get this pissed. I love you.

He forced a smile and said, "I love you too, but you have me nervous now."

Denim cupped his face so they could look each other in the eyes. "Antoine, I'm being serious now. It was a joke, and I promise not to marry Dre' until after we graduate from college. I'm so glad you're home."

He smiled and kissed her forehead. "I'm glad I'm home too, but I'm still going to have a little chat with that playboy Dre'."

They started walking together toward the exit.

Denim giggled and repeated, "It was a joke!"

"Come on, let's get out of here so we can find Dre'."

Denim giggled all the way to the car.

Antoine was somewhat relieved to find out his sister had played a joke on him, but he was serious about finding Dre'. He drove by his house, but he wasn't at home.

Denim knew he was at the youth center teaching art to the neighborhood kids, but she wasn't going to reveal that bit of information to her brother. She knew Antoine would eventually run into Dre', but until then she had plenty of time to fill him in on her joke, so he won't get caught off guard.

Chapter Six

Kane and her brothers were excited to get new clothes. They made their way to the parking lot with their shopping bags and climbed inside their father's vehicle.

"Who's hungry?" Myron asked.

"We are!" the boys yelled in unison. "We want pizza!"

"We're not eating pizza on Sunday. I want to have a nutritious meal with all the fixings," Myron announced as he pulled into traffic. "What about you, Kane? What do you have a taste for?"

"I like everything, Daddy. It doesn't matter to me where we go and long as we're together."

Myron's heart filled with joy upon seeing his family so happy. They hadn't had much to be happy about lately, but he was determined to turn things around for the whole family.

"OK! We're going to Gideon's. I'm craving a prime rib, and as you guys know, they have everything."

"I love their salads and rolls," Kane said.

"I like their hot fudge cake and ice cream," Justin stated.

"Can Momma go?" Christian asked with a timid voice.

Kane glanced over at her father, who smiled. Myron knew how sensitive his youngest son was with respect to his mother, so he wanted to make sure he kept the mood as upbeat as possible.

"She can't come today, son, maybe some other time. OK?"

"OK," he replied softly.

Kane reached over and took her father's hand into hers. "Thanks for letting me go shopping with Denim, Daddy."

"You're a teenage girl. I understand you need to spend time with your friends. I would like the opportunity to meet her parents though."

"I'm sure they won't mind." Kane pulled out her cell phone and sent Denim a text message.

Within seconds she received a reply telling Kane and her family it was fine for them to come by after they finished their dinner. This warmed Kane's heart because she now had a friend within walking distance of her house. It didn't hurt that Denim had a car, which meant Kane would have more of an opportunity to go to ball games, movies, and just hang out with other teens her age.

"Daddy, Denim said it was OK for us to come by after dinner to meet her parents."

Myron pulled into the restaurant parking lot and said, "That's perfect. Come on, you guys, let's eat. My mouth is watering for that prime rib."

Kane helped Justin out of the car. "You love your steaks, huh, Daddy?"

"Without a doubt, sweetheart," he replied. "I'm going to let you taste it, and you'll see what I mean."

They entered the restaurant and were immediately escorted to a table, where they enjoyed a delicious meal while catching up on each others lives.

Yolanda rolled over in bed and frowned when the sunrays interrupted her sleep. She put the pillow over her head to block out the rays, but it wasn't working. She sat up on the side of the bed to gather her thoughts. Her head was pounding from all the alcohol and other drugs she had consumed the night before.

She looked over her shoulder and noticed that

Leon was snoring and cuddled up with another woman. She didn't remember much about the night before, not that she did most nights.

"What the hell is this bitch doing in my bed?" Yolanda screamed, waking them out their drunken slumber.

Leon opened one eye and said, "Shut up with all that noise! Can't a brother get some sleep around here?"

"Hell, no! I'm not going to keep putting up with your mess," Yolanda yelled as the woman eased out of bed and into the bathroom. "This is my house too, and I'm not having it."

Before she could open her mouth again, Leon slapped her hard across the face, knocking her onto the floor. He stood over her and kicked her hard in the ribs just as the other young woman came out of the bathroom fully dressed.

He looked over at her and asked, "Where do you think you're going?"

She waved him off and said, "This is not my scene. I'm out of here."

"You don't leave until I say you can leave," he yelled at her. "Sit your ass down in the kitchen and wait until I handle this."

As the woman made her way into the kitchen,

Leon kicked Yolanda again. "Don't you ever disrespect me again in my own house! Now get up and go clean yourself up and fix me some breakfast."

Yolanda groaned in pain as she struggled to breathe as he kicked the wind out of her. This is what her life had been reduced to—Leon's own personal possession, and punching bag.

She pulled herself off the floor and over to her purse, from which she pulled out a .22-caliber handgun and pointed it at him.

"You bastard! You think you can treat me like this and get away with it?" Yolanda's hand was shaking as she aimed the gun at him.

Leon laughed. "Oh you're going to shoot me after all I've done for you?" He took a few steps toward her.

She wiped her eyes to clear her vision. "Stay away from me, Leon, or I swear to God, I will put a bullet in you."

Leon took a few more steps toward her and said, "You don't have it in you, babe. You're a little rich girl from the suburbs. You couldn't be a hood chick if you wanted to. Now put that gun down and make me some bacon and eggs, and I'll forget all about this."

"No!" Yolanda yelled. "I'm sick of you disrespecting me! I'm supposed to be your woman!"

"You are my woman, Yo-Yo. Look, I'm sorry I hit you. Now come on and get some breakfast." Leon was only a few feet from her now and almost within reach of the gun.

Yolanda shook her head. "You're going to stop passing me off to your friends too."

"That's cool," he replied, his hands up in defense. "I only did it to see if you had my back. Because of you, we're making a lot more money now. You did good, baby."

"What about that woman you had in our bed?"

With a wave of the hand, Leon said, "She don't mean anything to me. Look, I made a bad choice. It's not like you weren't with me too. I'm sorry, OK. Put the gun down."

As Yolanda reluctantly lowered the gun, Leon snatched it out of her hand and aimed it at her.

"Bitch! You've done lost your mind, pulling a gun on me. Now you have to pay."

Yolanda's eyes widened as Leon aimed the gun at her and pulled the trigger. She felt as if her leg was on fire as she fell to the ground.

As Leon stood over her and aimed the gun at her head, his partner Marcus rushed into the room upon hearing the commotion.

He yelled at his partner, "Leon! You don't need this kind of heat. Whatever she did, let it go!"

Leon handed Marcus the gun and said, "It's just a flesh wound anyway. She'll be all right. Clean her up and put her to bed for me."

Yolanda sobbed as the large man picked her up and carried her naked body into the bathroom to tend to her wound.

In the kitchen, Leon gave his other girl a kiss and pat on the backside.

"I heard a gunshot, Leon. What's going on?"

He pulled a container of orange juice out of the refrigerator. "Nothing for you to worry your pretty little head about."

"Are you going to take me home? I'm ready to get out of here."

"I thought you were going to stay and party with me today?" Leon wrapped his arms around her waist.

"I'm not so sure about this setup, Leon. You said you want me to be your girl, but it looks like you already have one. I'm not trying to be second behind any woman."

Leon cupped her face and kissed her on the lips. "Are you going to tell me you didn't enjoy yourself last night?"

"I was wasted, Leon. I would've enjoyed almost anything. Look, take me home and let me think about it. If I'm interested, you'll be the first to know."

Leon frowned. He wasn't used to a woman giving him an ultimatum and didn't like it one bit. "I have a better idea. Step!" he yelled as he slammed the refrigerator door closed. "You don't tell me what to do. You're too skinny for me anyway. Just step!"

The woman marched toward the front door and quickly exited, leaving the drama, drugs, and Leon behind her.

Inside the bathroom, Leon's partner, Marcus, helped Yolanda into a robe before dressing her wound. Modesty had gone out the window the moment Leon ordered him to take care of her, and in all honesty, she was glad it was Marcus and not any of the other guys he normally had hanging around.

"Thank you," she whispered through her pain.

Marcus looked at her and said, "What were you thinking when you pulled that gun on him? You know he's crazy."

Yolanda started sobbing. "I didn't think he would shoot me."

Marcus poured some peroxide over the wound and started wrapping it up in gauze. "Why are you still here, Yolanda? This life is not you."

She gritted her teeth. "Why are you here?"

"My reason is strictly business. What's your excuse?" Marcus shook his head.

"He said I owed him," Yolanda said, wiping her eyes. "He'll never let me leave."

Marcus taped the gauze and said, "I don't see any locks on the door. He's not holding you hostage."

"I don't have anywhere else to go," she answered softly. "My husband won't let me come home or near my children."

Marcus stood and opened the door to leave, but before closing the door, he said, "Look, Yolanda, you're a beautiful, intelligent chick. Get off the stuff and get your life together because this is not for you. If you did that, maybe your old man will let you back in."

"Marcus?"

He turned to her and asked, "What's up, Yolanda?"

"Could you give me something for the pain and help me back into bed?"

Marcus stared into her weak eyes. "I'll give you something, but it won't be what you're used to. It'll be legit. Can you handle that?"

She nodded in silence.

"Cool. First, let me help you with a shower. Then I'll get you something for the pain."

Yolanda smiled. "Thank you."

"You're welcome." Marcus turned on the shower.

"I'll go get the pain medication. By the time I get back, the water should be hot enough for you to get in."

Marcus returned seconds later with a couple of oxycodone pills and a Pepsi. Yolanda quickly gulped the pills down and handed the Pepsi to him.

"Eat this so you'll have a little something on your stomach," he instructed her.

Yolanda took the bread out of his hand and quickly ate it. She was amazed by his attentiveness, especially when he taped a garbage bag over her wound to keep it from getting wet and helped her in the shower.

"Are you cool with me being in here, Yolanda?" Marcus asked.

While bracing herself against his strong frame, she said, "Somebody has to help me. Besides, I'm sure I don't have anything you haven't seen before."

Yolanda was having a hard time standing. The medicine hadn't kicked in yet, so Marcus had to decide whether to cut the shower before it got started or help her. Within seconds he slowly stepped into the shower fully dressed, startling her.

"What are you doing?" she asked. "Your clothes are getting wet."

"I have other clothes," he replied casually. "Right now you need help."

Marcus made her feel calm and gave her a sense of security as he lathered her body. He didn't want to have any misunderstanding with Leon, so he made the shower as quick as possible.

Yolanda was starting to zone out as he turned off the water and stepped out onto the rug and grabbed a towel. As she looked into his eyes, she whispered, "How could I ever thank you?"

Marcus gently dried her body and wrapped the towel around her and sat her in a chair. "I've already told you," he reminded her. "Can you sit here while I change your bed?"

She nodded and watched as he quickly changed the bed. Once he had fresh, clean linens on the bed, he opened the closet and pulled one of Leon's shirts off the hanger and helped her into it. He picked her up and laid her on the sheets and pulled the comforter over her body.

Yolanda was almost unconscious, but she was still coherent enough to grab his hand.

"Can I get you anything else?" he asked before leaving the room.

Tears rolled out of her eyes as she was unable to speak, so she shook her head instead.

He smiled and said, "You're welcome. Get some sleep while I go get out of these wet clothes."

Yolanda closed her eyes as Marcus exited the bedroom.

Marcus met Leon in the hallway with a bottle of beer in his hand.

"Why are your clothes wet?" Leon asked before taking a sip of beer.

"You asked me to clean up your girl," he responded. "She's clean now, and I gave her something for the pain, so she's asleep."

Leon patted his friend on the shoulders and said, "Thanks, bro. I knew I could count on you."

"What you did was foul." Marcus said as he stepped around Leon. "She didn't deserve that bull."

"Maybe not." Leon chuckled. "But I bet she won't pull another gun on me."

Marcus didn't see the humor in Leon's statement. He wanted to leave, but he didn't want to leave Yolanda at the mercy of Leon.

"Whatever, Leon. Look, I'm going to run home and change clothes. Yolanda will be asleep for a while, so let her sleep. I don't want her wound to get infected, so I'm going to get her an antibiotic while I'm out. When I get back we have some business to discuss, so keep your head clear."

Leon smiled and said, "No doubt. I appreciate you looking out."

Marcus exited the house and quickly drove off. As he drove out of the neighborhood, he didn't understand at first why he was feeling the way he was, but it quickly became clear to him. Yolanda had made a strong impression on him. In fact she'd made an impression on him the first time he'd laid eyes on her, but she was Leon's girl and he didn't want to cross that boundary, even though he knew Leon didn't give a damn about her. All he could do now was watch over her from afar. He was hoping she would take his advice and get out as soon as possible.

Chapter Seven

Denim was studying for an upcoming World History test but was distracted when she heard laughter from outside. She sat her book on the bed and looked out of her bedroom window and spotted Kane throwing a baseball to Justin in her backyard. They'd had a great time hanging out at the mall a few days ago.

Today, she was going over to Kane's house for game night. It was great to have a friend who lived within walking distance. Patrice was her best friend, but she lived about twenty minutes away, not to mention her hands were full with Alejandro.

Denim watched Kane and her brother for a few minutes before deciding to raise the window.

"You have a good arm, Justin," she called out to him.

Justin looked up and smiled when he saw

Denim. He had developed quite a crush on her, and it was very obvious.

"Thank you, Denim," he answered. "Do you want to come down and throw the ball with me? Kane throws like a girl."

Kane giggled and threw her baseball glove at her brother. "You have a lot of nerve, you rat! You weren't saying that a few minutes ago when I threw you some heat."

Justin ignored his sister and walked closer to the fence that separated their yards. He looked up at Denim with a huge grin on his face and asked, "What time are you coming over? I can't wait to play the Wii with you."

"I can't wait to play with you either. Make sure you bring your A game because I'm bringing mine," Denim replied. "Are we still on for five o'clock?"

"You can come any time, Denim, even now, if you want to. We're just hanging out."

"I'm studying for a test right now, but I can come over when I'm done.

"Great!" Justin yelled as he ran across the yard and into the house.

Denim and Kane laughed.

"You do know that my brother is in love with you, don't you?" Kane asked.

"He's sweet," Denim replied. "I can tell he has a

crush on me, but don't worry, I'll let him down easy."

Kane laughed. "Good luck with that one. Go finish studying, and call when you're on your way over."

Denim slowly lowered the window and said, "I will." She picked up her diary and made a small, yet comical note:

I'm going to have to let Dre' know he has some serious competition. My neighbor Justin, who's eleven years old, is adorable, and has a small crush on me. I'm going over for game night with him, his brother Christian, and Kane. It should be fun.
Smooches!
D

A few hours later, Antoine walked Denim around the block to Kane's house, where he met Kane's father and brothers. He even stayed for one game of ping-pong before leaving them to their fun. He jogged back around to his house so he could go meet friends at a local bar and grill for hot wings and beer.

Right then, Dre' pulled into the driveway and parked beside his car. With a smile on his face, Dre' climbed out of his car and walked over to Antoine to give him a brotherly greeting.

"What's up, Antoine?" he said. "Dang! You're starting to look like a real lawyer. D.C. has been good to you. You're looking all GQ and thangs."

Antoine grabbed Dre' by the collar and said, "Get in the car. I need to talk to you."

Dre' backed away with a grin on his face. "You look a little tense, bro. Maybe we should catch up on old times some other day."

"I'm not tense." Antoine smiled. "I've been trying to track you down for a couple of days. I know Denim told you I was looking for you."

"She may have, but she told you she was just joking."

"I don't believe her." Antoine pointed his finger at Dre'. "Therefore I want to talk to you."

"Why won't you believe her?" Dre' asked in a stronger tone.

He wasn't afraid of Antoine. He knew he was just being protective of his sister. They'd had meetings like this before, and he respected Antoine for coming to him man to man, but it wasn't going to change his relationship with Denim or scare him off.

Antoine opened the car door. "We'll cover that in due time. Let's take a ride."

Dre' looked at his watch. "You know I'd love to, but I really need to—"

Antoine yelled, "Get in the damn car, Dre'!"

"Whatever, man," Dre' said in a grumbling tone as he climbed into the passenger side of the car.

Antoine backed out of the driveway and headed down the road. He looked over at Dre'. "I hope you and Denim don't think we're going to let you two get married before you go to college. You haven't lived your lives yet or dated other people. Marriage that young is a mistake."

Dre' fumbled with the radio dial as he listened to Antoine. He'd heard this all before. But the facts were, he wasn't interested in dating anyone else, and if he and Denim wanted to get married at eighteen, they would.

"Are you listening to me, Dre'?"

"I heard you, Antoine. Damn! Why are you being so hostile?"

Antoine brought the car to a stop at a traffic light. "Because I love my sister, and I don't want her to regret things later. First comes marriage then children you can't afford."

Dre' looked over at Antoine and smiled. The thought of children with Denim always warmed his heart.

"The light's green," he pointed out to Antoine,

who was so caught up in their conversation, he forgot where he was.

Antoine pulled through the light and continued their conversation. "Look, I like you, and I know all about being in love. Once you guys finish college, if you want to get married, you have my blessings, but until then, don't even think about it."

Dre' patted Antoine on the shoulders and jokingly said, "I appreciate that, brother-in-law. I'll talk it over with Denim and let you know what we decide."

"Smart ass!"

Dre' burst out laughing. "Where are you taking me anyway?"

"I'm meeting some friends."

"But I was going to see Denim. She's going to wonder where I am."

"You should've called first because Denim's not at home," Antoine said as he pulled into the parking lot of the restaurant.

"That's cool. She told me she might go over Kane's house."

Antoine turned the ignition off and said, "Listen, Dre', I have nothing against you dating my sister, as long as you respect her. She's obviously into you and happy, so I have to accept it. I have no doubt that you're going to be successful with basketball.

You're a talented artist and a good student. All I ask is that you don't string my sister along if you get to a point to where you want to date other girls."

"I told you I'm not interested in other girls."

The two of them climbed out of the car and walked across the parking lot to the restaurant.

"You say that now, but once you get in college and all those fine girls start cuddling up to you, it might change your mind."

Dre' grabbed Antoine by the arm, stopping him. He looked him in the eyes and, with serious conviction, said, "I don't think you understand me when I say I'm not interested in any other girls. I go to school with fine chicks now and they try everything under the sun to get me to cheat on Denim, but I won't. My heart is in one place, and that's with your sister. So, to hopefully settle this once and for all, let me assure you that we have no plans of getting married before we graduate from college, but if we change our minds, there's nothing you can do about it."

"Wait a second, Dre'. You seem—"

"No, you wait, Antoine!" Dre' yelled, interrupting him. "This little bum-rush you tried to do to intimidate me is not going to work. I respect you as Denim's brother, but I love her, and she loves me.

It's our life, and we're going live it our way. So butt out!"

Antoine stared at Dre'. They'd always been able to talk without things getting out of control. But Dre' was right about one thing. He wasn't going to intimidate Dre', and in all honesty, that wasn't his intention. He just wanted to talk to him to be assured that they would wait until after college before getting married. He realized he was at fault and had let his emotion get the better of him, causing him to approach Dre' the wrong way.

Maybe it was because his sister was growing up, and the way the young couple looked at each other. Maybe seeing them affectionate reminded him of just how much Danielle meant to him. He loved her and didn't want to lose her, and he could sense she was ready to make their relationship more permanent. He'd been stalling, telling her his career wasn't where he wanted it to be, that they should wait a little bit before getting married.

The truth was, he was scared like most men. Except for Dre'. He had a plan and knew exactly who and what he wanted in life, which was unusual for most guys his age.

"Dre', calm down. I'm not trying to give you a hard time. In fact, I'm glad my sister is with you,"

Antoine explained. "I just have to be sure you and Denim have your heads on straight. Are we cool?"

Dre' looked down at Antoine's extended hand. He shook it, gave him a hug, and said, "Yeah, we're cool."

Antoine opened the door to the restaurant. "Come on, let's eat."

"You're still buying, right?" Dre' asked, with a huge smile on his face.

"Yeah, I got you," Antoine said, and they made their way over to a table to join Antoine's friends, Allen and Derrick."

Chapter Eight

Yolanda woke up shivering, her clothing soaked with sweat. Her leg felt like someone was holding a hot poker to it. She opened her eyes and saw the ceiling fan circulating above her. The house was quiet, signaling to her that Leon was nowhere around. She needed to go to the bathroom, but her leg was throbbing.

As she reached over to the nightstand for a glass of water, she knocked the telephone onto the floor. Seconds later the door opened, and she saw someone in the doorway.

"What are you doing, Yolanda?"

She rubbed her eyes to clear her vision. "Leon?"

The man walked closer. "No, it's not Leon. It's Marcus. How are you feeling?"

"Besides my bladder about to burst, my leg feels

like it's on fire. And I'm cold one minute and hot the next."

Marcus scooped her up in his arms. "Let's get you to the bathroom first. We'll deal with the rest in a second."

Yolanda held onto Marcus's neck as he carried her into the bathroom and sat her down. Before walking out of the bathroom, he said, "Let me know when you're done. I'll be right outside."

She smiled and said, "Thank you."

A few seconds later, Yolanda opened the bathroom door. "I'm ready."

Marcus scooped her back up into his arms and sat her on the foot of the bed. "I think your leg might be infected," he said. "Are you allergic to any medicine?"

She thought for a second and said, "Not that I know of."

He pulled his cell phone out of his pocket. "You need some antibiotics. If I take you to the hospital, they'll call the police, and I'm not trying to deal with any heat. I know someone who makes house calls. I left a message earlier, I'll try again. ."

Yolanda looked up into his eyes. "Where's Leon?"

"Good question. He asked me to meet him here, but when I got here, the door was unlocked with you in here by yourself."

"That bastard!"

Marcus laughed and said, "It's about time you got angry."

Yolanda burst into tears.

"Do you want to get out of here, Yolanda?"

"I don't have anywhere to go," she replied through her sobs.

"You do now." Marcus opened the closet and tossed an empty suitcase on the bed. "I'm getting you out of here."

She knocked the suitcase on the floor. "Leon would see me dead before he'll let me go."

Marcus raised his shirt, revealing his 9 mm. "You let me worry about Leon. Get your things so we can get out of here. The doctor can look at you at my place."

Yolanda became nervous. "Your place? I can't stay with you."

"You can and you will. Now let's go. Leave whatever you have here. We can always buy more."

Marcus helped her into a trench coat and scooped her up into his arms. He maneuvered down the hallway, but when he got to the front door, he heard a car door.

"It's him!" Yolanda yelled.

"Calm down, Yolanda, and follow my lead."

Leon opened the front door and looked at the couple, a frown on his face. "What's going on?"

"Yolanda's running a fever. I need to get her to the doctor."

"You're not taking her to the doctor!" Leon slammed the door. "If they see that bullet hole, they'll file a police report."

Marcus sat Yolanda down in a chair. "I'm not stupid, Leon," he said. "I know all about discretion."

Leon walked into the kitchen and poured himself a glass of liquor and swallowed it. "Are you cool with this, Yolanda?"

"My leg is killing me. I need a doctor."

"Cool. You seem to be in good hands. You have my permission to have her checked out."

Marcus picked Yolanda up and headed out the door without responding. He quickly loaded her into his car and pulled out of the driveway.

"That was close," Yolanda said as she shifted in her seat. "My leg feels like it's on fire."

"You'll feel better shortly. I promise." Marcus pulled out his cell phone and made a call.

"Hey, it's me. I need a favor. My friend got hurt and I think she has an infection. Can you meet me at the townhouse?"

Yolanda listened to Marcus's conversation, not

knowing who he was talking to. At this point, all she wanted was relief from her pain, and assurance she wasn't going to die from the gunshot. After he hung up his cell phone, she asked, "Who was that?"

He looked over at her and said, "A friend. Just relax. You'll be feeling better in little or no time. OK?"

She nodded and closed her eyes. The sooner she was free of her pain and Leon, the better. Maybe escaping his clutches wasn't as bad as she thought it was going to be. At least having Marcus on her side was a start, but she wondered what he was going to want in return.

"We're here," Marcus said, waking Yolanda from her short nap.

When she opened her eyes, she could see they were pulling into the garage. "Is this your place?" she asked as he shut off the motor and climbed out of the car.

"Yes, it's mine. Hold on a second while I unlock the door." Marcus quickly opened the door and retrieved his new houseguest.

Inside the house, he laid her on the sofa and pulled a blanket over her body.

"You need to eat. I'll fix you a bowl of soup while we wait on my friend to arrive."

Yolanda sat up and asked, "Who exactly is this friend, Marcus?"

He pulled a can of soup out of the cabinet and smiled. "It's just a friend, Yolanda. Someone who'll be able to take your pain away and get you back on your feet."

"What do you want in return for all your generosity?"

He pulled the bowl out of the microwave and handed it to her. "I'm not like Leon."

She blew the soup to try and cool it down. "I'm glad."

Seconds later, there was a soft knock on the door, startling Yolanda.

"Sit tight. That's probably the doctor." Marcus disappeared into the living room and returned with an older gentleman following him.

"Yolanda, this is Doctor King. Doctor King, this is my friend, Yolanda."

The doctor greeted Yolanda and sat his medical bag on the coffee table. "I hear you have an injury to your leg," he said as he pulled back the blanket to examine her.

"My boyfriend shot me. Can you give me something for the pain, Doc? My leg feels like it's on fire."

The doctor glanced over at Marcus before removing the bandage. "Marcus, tells me you're dealing with somewhat of an addiction. What are you hooked on?"

Embarrassed, she whispered, "Coke."

"You know you're killing yourself, right?" Dr. King put on some latex gloves and surveyed the wound. "When's the last time you got high?"

"Not since I got shot. Listen, I don't need a lecture, Doc. Just give me something for the pain."

"Your concern should be with your heart stopping from the heavy drug use or the infection that could be setting up in your body right now," he answered with a firm tone.

"This is some bull!" Yolanda yelled. "My leg is throbbing."

Marcus walked over to Yolanda. "Calm down, woman, and let the man do his job."

The doctor took Yolanda's hands into his and stared into her eyes. "I'm going to give you something to take the edge off, but if you really want to get better, I can help you with that too. You're a beautiful young woman, and if you go anywhere near that stuff again, you could die. You don't want that, do you?"

"No, sir," she answered softly.

"That's what I wanted to hear. It's not going to be easy, and your body is going to go through hell, but you will get through it. Marcus is a good man, and he'll be here to help you transition. Are you ready?"

She nodded and whispered, "Yes, sir."

The doctor thoroughly cleaned the wound, gave her an antibiotic shot, and re-bandaged her leg.

Before finishing up, he gave her a shot for pain. He removed his gloves and said, "That should take care of her for now. If things don't improve over the next forty-eight hours, give me a call. I'll also give you some meds to help with her rehab. Are you sure about this, Marcus?"

He shook the doctor's hand and said, "More than anything. She's worth it."

The doctor patted Marcus on the shoulders. "I'm proud of you, son, and I hope this works out the way you want it to."

Marcus smiled. "I'm sure it will," he said as he walked the doctor to the door.

When he returned to the living room, Yolanda was asleep. He picked her up and took her into his bedroom and gently tucked her in. They had a long, harsh road ahead of them, but he was determined to help her recover.

* * *

Across town, Leon paced the floor as he waited for Marcus to return with Yolanda. As he waited, he got angrier and angrier. They had business to discuss, and he didn't like his time or money being wasted. Just as he was about to call, Marcus walked in the door.

"What the hell took so long?" Leon yelled.

"Yolanda's really sick." Marcus headed straight for the refrigerator and pulled out a bottle of beer.

"Where is she?"

"She's in an underground clinic my friend runs just for situations like this," Marcus lied. "Don't worry, Leon, she's in good hands. I have some good people taking care of her. She'll be as good as new after her treatment."

Leon didn't have a choice but to deal with it. Marcus was a potential business partner with the kind of connections and deep pockets he'd always dreamed of. But he was unaware of the type of treatment Marcus had planned for her. If it was up to Leon, he'd keep Yolanda a junkie for as long as he could, and he couldn't wait for her to come home so he could put her to work. But Marcus would never let that happen.

* * *

Over the next several weeks Marcus would nurse Yolanda's fragile body and soul back to health. Her recovery was a rough experience, with the concomitant vomiting, cold sweats, insomnia, muscle pain, and relentless diarrhea, and she was irritable and depressed.

But Marcus had seen that Yolanda had all the capabilities of becoming the woman she used to be, and he vowed to revitalize the desirable woman hidden inside.

Marcus himself went through some unexpected changes as well. He had fallen in love with her and couldn't see himself living without her.

Three months later, the cravings were gone, and Yolanda was smiling again. Marcus had fallen hard for Yolanda, and he was hoping she felt the same way about him. But he didn't want to pressure her. Her mind and body were still fragile, and he wanted to maintain her progress without any distraction.

In the meantime, he was more determined than ever to finish his business with Leon before revealing his true feelings to Yolanda. She couldn't handle any stress right now, and he would treat her with the utmost respect, while showering her with nothing but tender, loving care.

Sleeping in the spare bedroom had been difficult—Yolanda was a sexy woman with an amazing body—but he would continue to be a gentleman until she recovered fully.

Chapter Nine

Denim pulled out of her driveway and pulled up in front of Kane's house just as she was exiting the house with her family.

"Good morning, Mr. Alexander. Hey, guys."

Kane's dad opened his car door and said, "Good morning, Denim."

Denim climbed out of the car and gave Christian and Justin a hug. "Hey, boys."

All they could do was smile and blush.

"I guess you're on your way to school too, huh?" Kane asked as she put her book bag in the car.

"You know it."

"Hey, guys, we have to go," her father announced. "Kane, you and Denim can chat this evening. I don't want to be late for work."

"Mr. Alexander, if it's OK with you, I can drop Kane off at school. It's on my way."

Kane attended a private school a couple of miles from Langley High called Kenmore Academy.

Myron started the vehicle and asked, "Are you sure? I don't want it to be an inconvenience."

"It's fine, Mr. Alexander. She can ride home with me too."

"Thank you, Denim. You two need to get going, so you won't be late."

Happy, Kane quickly grabbed her book bag and made her way over to Denim's Mustang. "Thanks for the ride, Denim. I was getting tired of my dad driving me to school. I can't wait until I get my license."

As Denim pulled away from the curb, she said, "I bet. I love driving to school."

Kane looked around the interior of the vehicle. "Nice leather seats."

"Thanks. It used to be my dad's car. He had it restored for me."

"That's so cool."

"How do you like wearing uniforms to school every day?" Denim asked after she pulled up at a traffic light.

"It's OK. I'm used to it."

Denim looked at Kane's attire. "I guess it's not so bad, but I don't think I could wear a skirt every day."

Kane laughed. "You don't have to. We have khaki pants and shorts that come in navy too. I like not having to decide what to wear each day, but some days I do miss wearing jeans."

"I bet. So are there any cute boys at your school?"

Kane giggled, "There's a few, but I don't know why you're asking. You're spoken for."

"I'm not asking for me." Denim laughed. "I'm trying to find out if there's anybody you're interested in."

"There's a guy in one of my classes that's cute, but I think he's already dating someone."

"Have you ever talked to him?"

"A few times. Then there was a time when I accidentally walked into the boys' restroom. I think he was more shocked than I was."

"You're lying, Kane!" Denim yelled, clearly amused by Kane's unfortunate mistake.

"No, I'm serious. I had to go really bad, so I wasn't paying attention to the sign. When I walked in and saw those urinals, I froze. The boy basically rescued me from God knows what."

"Sounds like a good way to get a conversation going."

Kane blushed. "Not really. I was teased for nearly a month after that happened."

Denim pulled onto the campus of Kane's school.

"You should try to talk to him again. If you're nervous, maybe you try to talk to him over Facebook. He does have a Facebook page, doesn't he?"

"Yeah, he has one." Kane opened the car door and climbed out. "I'd better get going. Thanks for the ride."

"You're welcome. Don't forget . . . I'm picking you up after school."

"I won't."

Before Denim pulled away from the curb, a tall, handsome young man with dimples, green eyes, and wavy hair started walking in the direction of her car. "Who is that?" she asked.

Kane leaned into the car and whispered, "That's him."

"My, my, my, Kane Alexander, you're right. He is cute."

As the young man walked past Kane, he said, "Hey, Kane."

"Hey, Jalen."

Denim and Kane watched as the young man made his way toward the school entrance.

"Nice!" Denim acknowledged before putting her car in gear. "You need to check that, Kane. He's fine."

Kane giggled. "Whatever! I'll see you this afternoon. Drive carefully."

"I will, but don't forget what I said," Denim answered before driving away.

Kane hurried inside the building and made her way to her locker just as the first bell rang. She'd spent more time talking to Denim than she should have, and now she was about to be late to her first-period class.

After grabbing her trigonometry book, she slammed her locker door closed and rushed through the crowded hallway. Her class was on the second floor, so she had to hurry to avoid being late. She was making good time. As soon as she stepped through her classroom door, the second bell rang, saving her from a tardy.

Kane took her seat just as the teacher called the class to order. As Kane opened her notebook, she was interrupted when the girl sitting behind her tapped her on the shoulder. Kane turned around, and the girl passed her a small note. She opened it and saw that it was from Jalen, who always sat in the back corner of the room. She briefly made eye contact with him and then discreetly opened the note.

Who's your fly friend?

Kane knew not to answer his note during class. Their teacher was notorious for embarrassing students in the classroom, and she had been through enough embarrassment at Kenmore Academy. She tucked the note inside her notebook and decided to answer his question after class.

As soon as the bell rang, Jalen walked over to Kane and said, "Who was that girl who dropped you off this morning?"

"Why do you want to know?" She smiled. "Aren't you dating somebody?"

As they walked out into the hallway together, Jalen continued to quiz Kane.

"Maybe, but I still want to know who she is."

Kane stopped walking. "She has a boyfriend, Jalen, so there's no reason for you to care who she is. But, if you must know, she's my neighbor, Denim."

This information intrigued Jalen even more. "What high school does she go to?" he asked.

"She's a cheerleader at Langley, and her boyfriend—and I emphasize *boyfriend*—goes there too. He's their star basketball player. She's not available."

Jalen wrapped his arm around her shoulders, clearly taking her by surprise. "I respect that," he replied. "But I'd still like to meet her."

"Why?" Kane asked, slightly irritated.

"She's cute, and if she's your friend, that tells me she's sweet too."

"You're full of it, Jalen. And what makes you think I'm sweet?"

"I asked around."

As they continued down the hallway, Kane noticed the way girls were staring at them. She wasn't used to getting this type of attention. Jalen was known around school as the cute, nice guy who made good grades and was popular without being an athlete. A lot of girls dreamed of dating him, but rumor had it that the captain of the girl's basketball team had locked him down

"Once again, Jalen, aren't you dating someone?"

"I have friends," he said, blushing.

"That's not what I heard."

"And just what did you hear?"

"I heard that you and Fatima Fields were dating."

Jalen rubbed his chin before answering. "She's cool, and we've gone out a couple of times, but I'm still a single man."

Kane pushed his arm off her shoulders. "Well, I don't want to give Fatima or any of your other *friends* the wrong impression. I have to go to class, and so do you."

"Kane," he called out to her, stopping her in her tracks.

She turned slowly and put her hand on her hip. "Yes?"

He smiled and said, "Your friend is smoking hot, but I think you're hotter than her and any of the girls here."

Kane nearly fainted. Jalen had never acted like he was interested in her until today. Could it be that he was only being nice so he could get to Denim, or was he being genuine with his affection?

Jalen walked over to Kane and pulled out his cell phone. "Give me your number."

"I don't have time for this now," she replied before walking away. "If you want my number, meet me after school."

Jalen smiled and slid his cell phone back into his pocket. "That's a date," he said.

Kane finally made her way into her second-period class, but she was unable to concentrate. All she could think about was Jalen and the way he had come on to her. She didn't want to get too excited about the possibilities, but the thought made her body tingle.

After school, Kane exited the entrance and found Jalen on the steps talking to some guys.

When she walked past him, he quickly followed, calling out to her.

"Kane!"

She turned and waited for him at the bottom of the steps.

"I know you weren't leaving without giving me your number," he said.

"You looked busy, so I figured you could wait until tomorrow."

"No, I'm never too busy for you." He pulled his cell phone out of his pocket.

She looked into his handsome face and saw a twinkle in his eyes. He was blushing, and when he smiled, his dimples where mesmerizing. "Stop teasing me, Jalen."

"I'm not teasing you," he said with a serious look on his face. "I like you. I've always liked you."

As Kane recited her telephone number to Jalen, he punched the digits into his cell phone.

"Got it," he said. "That wasn't so painful, was it?"

Now it was Kane's turn to blush.

"Where's your cell? I want you to have my number too."

Kane pulled out her cell phone and gave it to him, so he could put his number in her address book.

Jalen handed the cell phone back to her and

said, "Feel free to call me any time. I'd love to get to know you better."

Just then Denim pulled up to the curb and blew her horn, and Kane waved at her.

Kane turned to Jalen. "I'd like that too. Look, if you still want to meet Denim, here's your chance."

Jalen pulled his book bag up on his shoulders. "Cool."

At the car, Denim exited the vehicle, so Kane could introduce her to Jalen. They shook hands, and then Denim said something that took Kane completely by surprise.

"Jalen, you and Kane should double-date with me and my boyfriend. I'm sure you'd like him."

Jalen looked over at Kane and noticed that her face had turned slightly red with embarrassment. "Double date, huh?" Jalen repeated. "Sounds good to me. What about you, Kane?"

"She'd love too," Denim said, answering for Kane, who seemed to be in shock. "Does Kane have your number?"

"Yeah, she has it."

"Great! She'll be in touch. It was nice meeting you, Jalen." Denim held out her hand to him once again and shook it. "We have to get going. See you around."

Kane turned to Jalen and opened her mouth, but

nothing came out. She was speechless and couldn't believe what Denim had done. She hadn't gone farther than exchanging cell phone numbers with Jalen, but Denim had pushed them up to another level.

Jalen opened the passenger side door for Kane, as Denim walked around to the driver's side. After the two got inside the car, he leaned down and gave Kane a kiss on the cheek. "See you tomorrow," he said as he stepped away from the car.

Denim put the car in drive and smiled as she pulled away from the curb.

"Kane?"

Kane stared straight ahead.

Denim pulled out onto the main street and called out to her once again but this time a little louder. "Kane!"

She turned to Denim and asked, "What just happened?"

Denim laughed out loud. "I just got you a date. You can thank me by buying me a double cheeseburger and fries. I'm starving!"

"Denim, I can't go out with Jalen. He's dating Fatima, an Amazon on the basketball team."

"He wasn't acting like he was dating somebody else. I saw him kiss you. Was it on the lips or the cheek?"

"It's not funny. You're going to get me beat up tomorrow."

Denim pulled into a local hamburger joint parking lot, a stop where a lot of students met after school to socialize, listen to music, and to get a juicy, thick burger.

"Nobody's going to touch you. Besides, cutie pie wasn't acting like he was dating somebody else. I think he really likes you."

They walked into the hamburger restaurant and saw students from several local high schools.

"I've never been in here before. Is it always like this?" Kane asked.

"Most of the time. I can't believe you've never been in here."

After they found a seat, Kane said, "My dad normally picks me up and we usually go straight home."

Denim looked up from the menu. "Well, you're riding with me now, so get used to it. There's a few other places we hang out at too."

"Who's *we*?" Kane asked.

"Me and my baby, Dre', and my *bff* Patrice and her boyfriend, DeMario. You'll meet them soon."

Denim and Kane recited their order to the waitress who came over to them. Then they continued to talk about their day at school, Jalen, and their futures. At one point in the conversation Kane became solemn when the topic of parents came up.

"So, have you seen or heard from your mom?" Denim asked.

Kane took a sip of her soda. "No, and I don't expect to. My dad took out a restraining order against her."

"Wow! I'm sorry to hear that."

"It's probably for the best. She really freaked me out. I've never been so embarrassed, and my dad was ready to kill her for what she did."

"You do know it's a sickness, right?" Denim said to her.

Kane let out a loud sigh. "Yeah, I know. I really miss her, but I don't like the person she's become."

Feeling the need to lighten the mood, Denim smiled and said, "Well, I hope she gets well soon, so you can have the mother/daughter relationship you deserve. I don't know what I would do without my mom."

"I never dreamed I would be going through something like this."

Denim gave her hand a squeeze. "The key thing, Kane, is that you will get through this. OK?"

"OK," she replied with a smile.

Minutes later, the waitress returned with their meals so they could indulge in a delicious teenager's delight.

Later, Denim made a solemn note in her diary:

My friend Kane is going through so much pain. I pray for her and her family every night. I also pray that her mother will be healed from her addiction soon.
Smooches,
D

Chapter Ten

It had been a long time since Kane had last seen her mother, but she was never far from her thoughts. She often wondered where she was and what she was doing and hoped that she was getting help for her addiction. In the meantime, Kane and her family had settled into her new neighborhood and had made new friends. Her friendship with Denim had grown closer, and when she wasn't hanging out with her and her friend Patrice, she was spending quality time with her family. Jalen was calling or texting her every day, and they had met at the movies a few times. She wanted her family to meet him in hopes that her father would allow her to go out on a real date with him. Luckily she was able to convince her dad to set aside some time this particular Saturday afternoon to meet

Jalen. She was nervous, yet excited, and prayed her brothers didn't embarrass her.

Jalen arrived twenty minutes early, and when Kane opened the door, he appeared just as nervous as she was. He looked handsome in his baggy jeans and an Akoo shirt.

"Hi, Jalen."

He couldn't speak at first. All he could do was smile.

"What are you staring at?" she asked.

He cleared his throat. "You. You're beautiful, Kane."

She blushed and said, "Thank you. You can come on in. My dad will be downstairs in a second. In the meantime, I'll introduce you to my brothers."

Jalen followed Kane into the family room, where they found Christian and Justin playing the Wii. Jalen continued to admire Kane's curves in her designer jeans and short yellow button-down jacket.

"Hey, guys, can you put the game on pause for a second? I want you to meet my friend, Jalen."

Christian was first to step forward to check out Jalen, who held his hand out and said, "What's up, li'l man?"

Christian shook his hand and asked, "Are you my sister's boyfriend?"

"Christian!" Kane yelled in embarrassment.

Jalen laughed and said, "It's cool, and I actually like the sound of it."

Kane couldn't believe her ears.

Justin stepped forward to meet Jalen. "I'm Justin," he said, and they shook each other's hands and continued to talk.

"Hello, Justin. You're pretty good with basketball. Do you play at school?"

"Yeah, I play."

"Do you start?" he asked.

"I'm a point guard. Do you want to play?"

Kane interrupted their conversation and said, "Maybe later, Justin. Jalen, would you like a Coke?"

"Sure," he replied as he followed her into the kitchen.

She opened the refrigerator and said, "I'm sorry about my brothers. They start playing that game and lose touch with reality."

Jalen accepted the Coke. "I understand. It's a guy thing. We're very competitive, no matter what we're playing."

Before she could respond, her father walked into the kitchen. He held out his hand and said, "You must be Jalen."

Jalen shook his hand and said, "Yes, sir."

"It's nice to finally meet you. I've heard a lot

about you from Kane. I appreciate you coming over so we could talk."

Talk? Kane thought to herself. She wanted her father to meet Jalen, not cross-examine him.

"Why don't we go into the family room so we can sit down?" Myron suggested. "Kane, bring the sandwich tray and drinks into the family room."

Kane watched her father and Jalen exit the kitchen before pulling out the tray of sub sandwiches. She also pulled a large bowl out of the cabinet and filled it with chips and took it into the family room. She sat the sandwiches and chips on the table and then went back for the sodas. Once she finished arranging the food, she sat down on the sofa next to Jalen, while her brothers continued to play the Wii.

"So, Jalen, Kane tells me you're an honors student at Kenmore."

"Yes, sir. My parents wouldn't have it any other way."

"What about sports?" Myron asked as he picked up a sandwich and placed it on his plate. "Do you play any?"

"Track is the only sport I participate in. I played little league baseball when I was younger, but I love track the most."

Myron smiled and asked, "Are you any good?"

Kane smiled and said, "He's the best on the team, Daddy."

"Oh really? What's your event?"

Jalen took a sip of his Coke. "I run the hundred, the four by one hundred, and the four by four hundred."

"That's great, Jalen. I was a sprinter as well when I was in high school, so I know the amount of conditioning that it takes to stay in shape."

"Yes, sir."

"You have to watch what you eat, and you can't get caught up in alcohol and drugs."

With that statement from her father, Kane realized the conversation was headed into a different direction.

"You're right, sir, and believe me when I say I wouldn't go near that stuff."

"I want to believe you, son, especially if you're thinking about dating my daughter. Kane means the world to me, and you do anything to hurt her, you'll have to answer to me."

Jalen sat his sandwich down and said, "Mr. Alexander, I really like Kane. I would never hurt her."

"You're teenagers. You don't mean to do a lot of

things, but it happens. I'm just letting you know
that Kane is my daughter, and I won't let you or
any boy disrespect or take advantage of her."

"Daddy, Jalen wouldn't do that."

"Sure, he would. He's a man. It's in our nature for
us to mess up with women."

Myron's comment made Jalen smile.

"Jalen, I'm not saying you're a bad kid or that
you're going to mess up with Kane. I was a
teenager once, so I know what's up. All I'm saying
is, do not go there with my daughter. Understood?"

"Understood, Mr. Alexander."

"Good! On that note, I'll let Kane go out with
you."

"Thank you, Daddy," Kane replied as she hugged
and kissed him.

"Yes, thank you, sir," Jalen answered.

"Great! Let's eat, play the Wii, and have some
fun."

The rest of the afternoon they enjoyed the sandwiches and playing the Wii. Myron even allowed
Jalen to take Kane out for dessert. It was a great
evening and one that Kane would always cherish.

Yolanda was finally healthy and off drugs, leaving her feeling like a new woman. To reward her
even more, Marcus treated her to a complete

makeover, including hair, nails, pedicure, and a new wardrobe. Since she'd been living with Marcus, she had gained ten pounds and had somehow fallen in love with her new roommate along the way. He had been so attentive and loving to her, and the main reason she had overcome her addiction.

Her fear of Leon had diminished when she discovered he had been arrested for drug trafficking, gun possession, and a variety of other federal charges, which gave him a life sentence. This was all possible because of an unlikely source and savior.

"Marcus, did you see where Leon was arrested for drug trafficking?" Yolanda asked when he entered the house. "I heard he was caught in some type of drug sting."

He sat his keys on the table. "Yeah, I heard, but there's something I need to talk to you about."

Yolanda put her hand over her heart and said, "What? Are you going to be arrested too? What about me? Am I in trouble too?"

Marcus took Yolanda by the hand and sat her down on the sofa. "Calm down, Yolanda. You're not in trouble, and neither am I."

In a panic she jumped up and yelled, "You conducted business with Leon! If the police got enough evidence to arrest him, it's only a matter of time before they come for us too!"

Marcus smiled and said, "It's OK, babe. I *am* the police. You're fine."

"How can it be OK? I used to live and do drugs with the man."

He smiled and cupped her face. "Yolanda, are you listening to me?"

"Yes, I'm listening."

"I'm an undercover federal agent. I'm the one who got the evidence on Leon to bust him."

Yolanda moved away from Marcus. "You've been lying to me?"

He walked over to her and said, "I lied to save you. You didn't deserve to be with a punk like Leon, or in jail, which is where you would've ended up. I couldn't let that happen."

Still shocked from Marcus's confession, she asked, "Why?"

"Because." He reached up and caressed her cheek.

She looked up into his eyes and asked, "Because what?"

"Can't you see that I'm in love with you?"

"I don't know what to believe anymore," she replied. "I don't even know who you really are. Is Marcus even your real name?"

"No, it's Devin. Devin Gardner."

"Wow! Another lie," she said, backing away from him.

"Are you going to stand here and say you don't feel anything between us, regardless of what my name is?"

"No, I'm not saying that," she replied as she put her hands over her eyes. "I'm saying I can't handle this right now."

He took her hands into his and placed it over her heart, "Yolanda, a name is just a name. Tell me what you feel inside."

"You've taken care of me when I didn't feel worthy," she said, tears filling her eyes. "And I don't know where I would be if it hadn't been for you."

"I did it for you . . . for us, Yolanda. Look me in the eyes and tell me you can't see that my feelings for you are genuine. All I'm asking is for you to give us a chance."

She thought to herself for a second and realized she was overreacting. She cupped his face and whispered, "I'm sorry I freaked out on you."

He hugged her waist and said, "Apology accepted."

She gave him a sensual kiss, and a sensation overtook her body like she never expected, and it felt fabulous.

"So are you going to give us a chance?"

She nodded and laid her head against his chest and said, "Yes, Marcus—Devin or whoever you are. I'll give us a chance."

He laughed and hugged her tighter picking her off the floor. He knew she loved him. Now they had one more hurdle to cross, which was her past.

Kane and Jalen walked into the restaurant, known for its colossal desserts, and sat down at a table. They couldn't wait to see what was on the menu.

"Do you like chocolate?" Jalen asked as he scanned the menu.

She looked at him with a twinkle in her eyes and said, "I like anything sweet. What about you?"

"Anything but coconut."

Kane looked down at the menu and said, "There's one with brownies, ice cream, caramel, whipped cream, shortbread, and cherries. How does that one sound?"

He closed his menu and said, "Order whatever you want. They're so big, we can split one."

The waitress came over to the table and took their order. While they waited, Jalen couldn't help but caress her soft hands.

"Your dad don't play, huh?"

"He's cool. He's just protective of me."

Jalen smiled and said, "He should be because I had a hard time keeping my hands to myself."

"Well, he's not here now. What do you want to do?" she asked in a challenging tone.

He eased over in the booth beside her and put his arm around her shoulders. "First on the list is a kiss."

Kane closed her eyes when Jalen leaned over and kissed her with his soft, warm lips. It felt heavenly, and she didn't want it to end.

"Kane Latrice Alexander!" Yolanda called out to her. "What the hell are you doing?"

The young couple was startled apart.

"Mom, what are you doing here?" Kane asked nervously.

"This is your mother?" Jalen asked.

Yolanda pointed her finger at Jalen. "Who are you? And why were you fondling my daughter?"

"Mom, please," Kane pleaded with her.

Devin walked over to the table. "What's going on here?"

"This boy was fondling my daughter."

Devin grabbed Yolanda by the shoulders and said, "Calm down, sweetheart. You're causing a scene, and you're scaring your daughter. Let's sit down and talk calmly, OK."

Reluctantly, Yolanda slid into the booth across from her daughter and Jalen, and Devin sat down with them as well.

Devin held out his hand to Kane and said, "I'm sorry we haven't been properly introduced. I'm Devin Gardner. You must be Kane. I'm a friend of your mother's. I'm sorry she reacted like this. It's just that she hasn't seen you in a while."

Kane looked into her mother's eyes and noticed the remarkable change in her appearance. Her hair was styled, and her makeup was flawless. In fact, she was stunning and looked nothing like she did the last time she'd seen her.

"Mom, you look so pretty."

"Thank you, sweetheart. I owe it all to Devin," she said as she hugged his waist. "He's helped me so much."

"That's great, Mom, but you know Dad has a restraining order against you. You're not supposed be anywhere around me."

"I know, but I had no idea I was going to see you here." Yolanda caressed her daughter's face. "I'm sorry for everything that I've put you and your brothers through. I love you guys and I can assure you that I'm much better and I'm getting my life together."

Embarrassed that Yolanda had revealed so much of her private life in front of Jalen, Kane decided to finish their conversation in private.

"Jalen, can you excuse us for a second? I haven't seen my mom in a long time, and I would like to talk to her in private. I'll explain later."

Jalen nodded, but before walking away, he kissed Kane on the cheek and said, "If you need me, I'll be outside."

"Thank you," she replied before turning back to her mother and the stranger accompanying her. "Listen, Mom, I'm glad you're better, and you do look great, so whatever you've done worked. All I want is to be able to have my mother back. I miss you."

"I miss you too, sweetheart, and I didn't mean to scream at you and your friend. It's just that I didn't expect to see you, and it's been such a long time. Is he your boyfriend?"

"Sort of. We just started dating. He's really a nice guy, Mom, and he wasn't fondling me. We were only kissing."

"I know, baby, but kissing leads to other things, and I don't think you're ready for that. I don't want you growing up too fast. You're my baby."

"I know, Mom, but I am sixteen"

Yolanda smiled. "Don't remind me. It seems like

yesterday that your father and I brought you home from the hospital."

Kane noticed the tears that filled her mother's eyes. "Mom, do you have a number where I can reach you? Maybe I can talk Daddy into canceling the restraining order so we can see you."

"I'll take care of that." Devin pulled out a piece of paper, wrote down his number, and handed it to Kane. "Your mother is my houseguest, so feel free to call her any time."

Kane looked down at the number and said, "Thank you."

"You know your mother is a wonderful woman, and I care about her very much. Nothing would make her happier than having you and your brothers back in her life."

"I'd like that too, but I don't think Dad will go for it."

Devin stood and then helped Yolanda out of her seat. "If you want to, you can give your father my number so we can talk," he said. "We're sorry we interrupted your date. He seems like a nice young man. Just remember what your mother told you, because she loves you."

"I will." Kane stood and hugged her mother. "I love you, Mom."

"I love you too, baby," Yolanda replied with a kiss to her daughter's forehead.

Yolanda and Devin decided to choose another restaurant to have dinner so Kane would feel comfortable on her date.

When Jalen returned to the table, Kane explained the bizarre situation between her and her mother. Jalen was supportive and assured her that she had no reason to be embarrassed. Life happens, and it was obvious she was better.

An hour or so later, Jalen took Kane home and ended their date with a hug and kiss.

Chapter Eleven

A day or two later, Kane shared her experience with Denim on the ride to school. Denim could see that the light in Kane's eyes was much brighter than it had been previously. Maybe she would be able to mend their damaged relationship after all. But it wasn't up to Kane, and her father was still unaware of their chance meeting.

"What are you going to do?" Denim asked. "Are you going to tell your dad about her?"

"I want to, but I'm afraid he's going to go ballistic. I mean, I want to be able to talk to my mom, but she's hurt him so bad, I don't think he wants to have anything to do with her."

"If she's off the drugs, he should let you guys see her. You do want to see her, don't you?"

"Of course, I do. I think she has a new boyfriend too, but he seems cool."

"Are your parents divorced yet?"

"My dad filed, but she has to sign off on it. Until now no one knew how to get in touch with her."

As Denim pulled up in front of Kenmore Academy, she asked, "Do you think your mom wants a divorce?"

"I'm not sure," Kane said, opening the car door. "But I believe their marriage is over. She seemed comfortable with the guy she was with now, and he looks decent, so we'll see."

"Take it one day at a time, Kane, but I think you need to talk to your dad. I'll see you this afternoon, and tell Jalen I said hello."

"Thanks, Denim, and drive carefully," she answered before closing the car door.

Yolanda was pacing the floor when Devin entered the house.

"Hey, baby. What's up?"

She hugged his neck and said, "I'm glad you're home.

"What's wrong?" he asked.

"I need to see my kids. Will you take me?"

He kissed her forehead and said, "Slow down, Yolanda. I knew seeing your daughter was going to affect you, but you're going to have to move slowly.

I'll help you any way I can, but there's something I need to know."

"What's that?"

"Are you still in love with your husband?"

Yolanda lowered her head and said, "I love him, but I'm not in love with him. We had grown apart even before I started doing the coke."

"What will you do if he wants you back?"

"We could never be like we were. He even looks at me differently. I damaged him, and believe me when I say he won't take chances with me again."

"I want you to be happy, Yolanda, so if being with your family will make you happy, I'll step out of the way."

She hugged his waist and said, "I'm happy here with you, but I need to be able to see my kids too."

"I know you do, but we're going to have to do this the right way, and the first thing we have to do is prove to your husband that you're clean and you need a job."

"I'm a real estate agent. That's what I do, but I don't know anyone who'll hire me."

"Then start your own agency. It's not going to be easy, but you have to start somewhere. Are you up for the challenge?"

"Yes, I'm ready."

"Good. We'll get through this together."

* * *

That afternoon Kane had Denim drop her off at her father's office instead of home. She wanted to talk to him about their mother, and couldn't wait until he got home.

"Mr. Alexander, your daughter is here to see you," the secretary said as she poked her head inside his office.

"What is she doing here?" Myron asked as he walked out into the reception area to greet her. "Kane? What's wrong?"

She stood and gave him a hug. "Hi, Daddy. I need to talk to you about something, and it couldn't wait until you got home."

"Sure, sweetheart. Come into my office."

Kane followed her father into his office, where he closed the door and offered her a seat.

"Do you want something to drink?"

"Yes, sir. A Pepsi if you have one," she replied.

Myron handed his daughter a Pepsi out of his dorm-size refrigerator. "Now what do you want to talk about?"

"Mom. I saw her the other day, and she looks wonderful. She's not on the drugs anymore, and I want to be able to see her. I miss her, and I know Christian and Justin will want to see her too."

Myron frowned. "Did she come to the house again?"

"No, Daddy. I saw her when Jalen took me out for dessert. She was at the same restaurant."

Myron walked over to the window and looked out on the busy street. "What makes you think she's not on the drugs anymore?"

"Daddy, she looks so pretty. Nothing like she did the last time I saw her. Can you cancel the restraining order? Please?"

Myron turned to his daughter and said, "I have to think about this, Kane. Your mother has done a lot of damage to this family. I won't let her do it again."

Kane pulled the piece of paper with the telephone number on it out of her purse and held it out to her father. "Here's her telephone number. She said you can call her to discuss being able to see us."

"She has a phone now?"

"Sort of, Dad. She was with a guy who said she was living with him."

Myron tucked the number in his pocket. "He's probably another drug dealer. That's all she hangs with."

"I don't think so, Daddy. This guy seemed on the

up-and-up, and he acted like he really cared about Mom. I think he was her boyfriend."

Hearing those words left a bitter taste in Myron's mouth. He still cared about his wife, but he was reluctant to believe she was off drugs. "You know I want you guys to be happy, right?"

"Yes, sir."

"Do you know what kind of chance I'll be taking by letting her back into our lives?"

Kane picked up his cell phone and said, "Why don't you call her and set up a meeting so you can see for yourself? All I want is to be able to see her. If you don't want her back, I understand, but I miss my mother."

Myron hugged his daughter. "I know you do. I'll call her, but I'm not making any promises."

"Thanks, Daddy."

Myron grabbed his jacket and said, "Let's get out of here. I need to pick the boys up from school anyway. We'll talk more about this at home."

Later that evening Yolanda cooked dinner for her and Devin. He was at work but was due home any minute. Her love for him was growing stronger each day, and she realized the risks he'd taken when he rescued her from Leon and allowed her to live with him. It wasn't just his career he was risking. He was risking his heart as well.

As she set the table, she was startled by the ringing of the telephone. She figured it was Devin calling to check on her, an everyday ritual when he was at work.

"Hello?" she answered.

"Yolanda, it's Myron."

"Myron?"

"Yeah, it's me. Kane told me she ran into you the other day. Now she's asking to see you."

"I want to see them too, Myron. I've made a lot of bad mistakes when it comes to my family, but I'm clean now, and I miss my children."

"You expect me to forget everything you've done just like that, huh?" Myron asked with an irritated tone.

"No, I don't expect you to forget, but I do expect you to forgive. I know I hurt you, Myron, and I'm sorry. I'm not asking for you to let me move back in. I'm just asking to see my children."

Myron sighed. "I don't know, Yolanda."

"Please? Why don't we have lunch tomorrow or something, so we can talk face to face? If you're still not convinced I'm serious about the children, my life, and staying healthy, I'll abide by your decision. Deal?"

"Deal," he answered. "Where do you want to meet?"

"You pick the place."

Myron called out the name of a restaurant, and after hanging up the telephone, he wondered if he was going to regret his decision. He knew he would have to go through with the meeting, for his daughter's sake and for his own sanity.

Myron was actually nervous about meeting his wife for lunch. He was afraid that his heart was going to override his mind and make him soft, but he knew he had to stand firm. He'd put his foot down when it came to his wife's addiction, to protect his children, and he carried no regrets for doing so.

He decided to have a drink just to calm his nerves, but it did nothing for him when he saw her walk in dressed in snug-fitting jeans and a stunning cobalt blue blouse. He stood and waved her over to the table. When she approached the table, he could see that Kane was right. Yolanda looked healthier than ever, and her curvy figure was undeniably pronounced.

"Hello, Myron, it's so nice to see you."

Myron pulled her chair out for her and said,

"Likewise. You look wonderful. Life has definitely changed for the better for you."

"I guess you can say that," she said, smiling. "You look great as well."

"Thank you," he answered, but what he really wanted to know was how she beat her addiction. "Yolanda, I hope you don't mind me asking, but how did you beat it?"

Yolanda took a sip of water and said, "Through the grace of God and a wonderful, wonderful, man who risked everything to help me. He was truly a godsend."

Myron started scanning the menu and asked without looking up, "Is it anyone I know?"

"No, he's actually a federal agent who saved me from that evil man who was keeping me high. He's in jail now, so I don't have to worry about him anymore. I just wish it could've happened sooner. You know?"

"Yeah, me too. I've missed you."

"I've missed you too."

The couple stared at each for a second as both of them reminisced about their life before the drugs, the pain, and the heartache.

"What do you want to order?" Myron asked, snapping himself and his wife back to reality.

"Soup and salad will be fine for me. I'm not

really hungry. I want to get this thing settled about the kids and the restraining order. I can't move forward with my life until we do. I love them, Myron, and I need them in my life."

"What about me? You haven't said a thing about us."

Yolanda let out a loud sigh. "You and I both know it's too late for us. You fell out of love with me a long time ago, thanks to me and my addiction. You're a good man, and I couldn't ask for a better father for our children. I called Anthony McKinney, and he told me you had some divorce papers for me to sign. Do you have them with you?"

Myron reached for Yolanda's hand and caressed it. "Can't we take a breath for a second?"

"I can't live with you looking at me the way you do," she said, placing her napkin in her lap. "There will always be that doubt in the back of your mind whether I've relapsed. We can't live like that. It's time we both started over fresh. Do you have the papers with you so I can sign them?"

"They're at the house. I'm happy you were able to recover, Yolanda. I've never wanted anything but the best for us. Kane was right when she said you were stunning. Whoever this guy is, he's worked wonders with you, not only physically but emotionally too. The light is back in your eyes and your smile."

"I appreciate that, Myron, because everyone deserves a second chance at life and love, and no matter what, I'll always love you."

About to choke up, Myron cleared his throat. "I'll always love you too."

"Thanks. I needed to hear that."

"I'll see what I can do about the restraining order, but I want to start out slow with the kids. Christian has been very despondent since you left. I believe he'll benefit the most by seeing you."

Tears filled Yolanda's eyes and started running down her cheeks. "Can I see them today?"

"I don't know about that, Yolanda. It's too short notice."

Yolanda gave Myron's hand a squeeze and said, "You know I don't like to beg, but I'm begging you. Please let me see my babies."

"Let me think about it over lunch, and I'll see."

The couple carried on a nice conversation over lunch, and once they finished, Myron did something he thought he would never do—trust his wife again.

He drove her back to his house, where they waited for the children to come in from school. He had sent Kane a text asking her to see if Denim would pick up the boys from school as well.

A couple of hours later, the three children stepped through the front door and froze. Christian burst into tears as he ran across the room and jumped into his mother's arms, and the room was soon filled with more tears, as Kane and Justin also cried upon seeing their mother.

Chapter Twelve

"Mom, are you here to stay?" Justin asked through his sobs.

Yolanda caressed his face and, through her tears, replied, "No, baby. Momma can't stay today. I just wanted to see you guys and to let you know that I'm not sick anymore."

Christian hugged her tighter and said, "Please don't leave."

Myron walked over to Christian and picked him up into his arms. "Christian, your mother is better, but she's still working some things out. We still have a lot of things to discuss before we decide where we go from here."

"But I want her to stay!" Christian yelled.

Justin added, "I want Mom to stay too."

Myron knew he was outnumbered, but he still wasn't ready to give in.

"Guys, let's take a breath for a second. We're all overwhelmed at seeing your mother after so long. Your mother and I have some legal matters we have to take care of before we can move forward."

Kane held her mother's hand and asked, "Daddy, can Mom stay tonight?"

Yolanda could see that Myron was backed into a corner, so she decided to rescue him. "Hold on a second, guys," she called out to them. "Nothing would make me happier than to be able to hold each and every one of you tonight, but I can't. I'm better, but I still have some obstacles to overcome before I'll be able to see you guys on a regular basis. Your father and I will work through things so we can spend time together. In the meantime, if you want to call, Kane has my number."

"Don't you want to be with us, Mom?" Justin asked.

"Of course, I do, Justin. I love you, but I have to fix things with your dad first. OK?"

"Yes, ma'am."

"I have to go, but I'll be back." Yolanda stood up. Then she hugged and kissed each one of the children before walking toward the door.

Myron picked up his keys and turned to the children. "I'll be back shortly. I have to take your mother back to her place. Kane, get them started on their homework. I'll pick up dinner on my way home."

Kane put her arms around her brothers and said, "Yes, sir. Good-bye, Mom."

"Good-bye."

It took Myron nearly twenty minutes to drive Yolanda back to Devin's townhouse. After he pulled into the driveway, he put the vehicle in park and looked over at her. "It really was good to see you, Yolanda."

"It was good seeing you too." Yolanda kissed his cheek. She then climbed out of the vehicle and walked around to the driver's side. "Myron, I want you to meet Devin sometime soon. It looks like this is going to be my home for a while, and I want you to be comfortable letting the kids come over if we can iron out all the red tape."

Myron stared at her without answering. He couldn't get over how great she looked. He scratched his head then asked, out of nowhere, "Are you happy with him, Yolanda?"

"I am," she said, blushing.

Myron put the vehicle in gear. "I'll talk to McKinney when I get home."

"Thank you, Myron. And speaking of McKinney,

did you remember to grab the divorce papers when we were at the house?"

Myron sighed as he pulled the papers out of his pocket.

"It's OK, Myron," Yolanda said, patting him on the hand. "We both know it's for the best."

Myron watched as Yolanda signed the papers and handed them back to him.

"Here you go. I won't fight you for custody of the children, but I would like visitation rights. Under the circumstances, I don't think I deserve joint custody."

Myron got out of the vehicle and pulled her into a loving embrace. "As long as you stay clean, you can have joint custody. They're your children too."

Yolanda couldn't believe her ears. After all she'd done to hurt their relationship, he still had a heart. "I want to thank you again for raising Kane and the boys."

"No. Thank *you* for caring enough about your children to get yourself right. Take care of yourself."

"I will."

Myron watched her as she walked up the sidewalk and disappeared into the house.

* * *

Yolanda put her purse on the hallway table and found Devin in the kitchen cooking. When they made eye contact, he immediately saw the tears in her eyes.

He pulled her into his arms and asked, "How did it go?"

"I got to see my kids," she said, hugging his neck.

"That's what you wanted, right?"

She looked into his eyes and said, "Yes, that's what I wanted, but it wouldn't have been possible without you."

Devin caressed her face. "Mission accomplished."

"I love you, Devin." Yolanda kissed him hard on the lips.

"I love you too, sweetheart."

Yolanda walked over to the stove, turned off the burners, and led him into the bedroom.

"Let's make it official. I never want to leave your arms, Devin Gardner."

He kissed her and said, "I second that motion."

When Myron returned home he had the unpleasant task of telling the children about the divorce and that their mother would not be coming home to live with them. Before they had a chance to react, he assured them that he wasn't going to alienate Yolanda from them. He promised them she would be in their lives, as long as she stayed healthy and was careful about the company she kept.

He hugged them and said, "We'll get through this together. You'll see."

"Daddy, I met Mom's new friend. He's really nice."

"I'll have to see for myself, but you're a great judge of character. If you say he's good, I believe you. Besides, he was the one who helped your mother get well."

"I know, Daddy! We can invite them over for Christian's birthday party."

"Please, Daddy," Christian begged.

"OK," he answered. "This is going to be an adjustment for all of us, but I have no doubt we'll be just fine."

"As long as I can visit Mom and she can visit me, I'll be cool," Kane responded.

Over the next week, Myron worked with his attorney and the courts to have the restraining order canceled. The judge was concerned about the grounds for the cancellation, but Myron assured the judge that he no longer felt threatened by Yolanda's addiction, that she had turned her life around. With assurance from Myron and his attorney, the judge dismissed the restraining order.

The following month, Kane and her family celebrated Christian's tenth birthday with a cookout in their backyard. Christian invited some friends from school, and Myron invited family and the Alexanders to be a part of the celebration. No one was more pleased than Kane when her mother and her friend Devin arrived with an arm full of presents.

"Mom!" Christian yelled as he ran and jumped into her arms.

"Happy birthday, baby!" Yolanda said as she hugged and kissed her youngest son. She sat him down. "I have someone I want you to meet. Devin, this is my youngest son, Christian. Christian, this is my good friend, Devin."

"It's nice to meet you, sir."

Devin leaned down and shook Christian's hand. "It's nice to finally meet you too."

Myron saw Yolanda and her friend enter the backyard, so he excused himself from the guests and walked over to greet them. He gave Yolanda a kiss on the cheek and said, "I'm glad you could make it, Yolanda."

"Me too. Myron, this is Devin, the man who saved my life. Devin, this is Myron."

Myron held out his hand to Devin, who happily greeted the father of Yolanda's children.

"I've heard a lot about you," Devin said.

"I'm sorry I haven't had the same pleasure, but I hope to get to know you."

Kane held on to Denim's hand and walked her over to her mother. "Mom, this is my friend, Denim. I'm sure you probably don't remember her. She was with me at McDonald's."

"*Denim*, that's a unique name. I'm sorry, I was a different person back then. If I said or did anything to hurt or embarrass you, I'm sorry. Can you ever forgive me?"

Denim shook Yolanda's hand. "Of course, I forgive you. I love your outfit."

"You do? I hope I'm not overdressed." Yolanda twirled around, modeling her pantsuit and three-inch sandals.

"You look perfect, Mom." Kane hugged her mother's waist. "Come on, so I can introduce you guys to Denim's parents."

Denim stood back and watched as Kane and her brothers loved on their mother and her friend

Devin. Devin even helped Kane's father grill the food. Later, she witnessed Mr. Alexander giving Devin a high-five after playing a game of horse-shoes. Things seemed to be falling into place, just like Kane and her family had hoped. In fact, it seemed as though she was going to have two fami-lies instead of one.

Kane walked over to Denim and said, "Guess what?"

"What?"

"Mom and Devin are engaged."

"Are you serious?"

"She has a ring and everything," Kane told her.

"How do you feel about it, Kane?"

Kane looked over at her mother, who was laugh-ing out loud and said, "She's happy, Denim. Look at her. Devin can't seem to take his hands and eyes off of her."

"Does your dad know?" Denim asked cautiously.

"Yeah, they told us together. He seems cool with it, but I know he still loves her. It's only a matter of time before he finds someone too."

Denim put her arm around Kane's shoulders. "I'm sure he will."

"Come on, Denim. We're getting ready to have a three-legged race.

"Just a second," Denim replied, reaching inside her purse and pulling out her diary. She then wrote:

Today I joined my neighbors in a birthday celebration for Christian, who turned ten years old today. Their family has gone through some tough trials and tribulations over the past year, but life always has a way of working things out for the better. My friend Kane didn't lose her mother to drugs after all, who's happy, healthy, and drug-free. She's also gained a friend and future stepfather, who's a police officer and seems to be a great role model for her and the boys. And Mr. Alexander appears to be happy in spite of their divorce. I have no doubt he'll find true love again, just like Ms. Yolanda did.

Smooches!

D

Epilogue

Denim and her family exchanged good-byes with the Alexanders before making their way out of the yard. It had been a wonderful birthday party and celebration to new beginnings for the family. As Denim and her family walked together, her cell phone rang, interrupting her tranquility. She didn't recognize the number on her caller ID, but she answered it anyway.

"Hello?"

"Is this Denim Mitchell?" the caller asked.

"Yes. May I ask who's calling?"

The young male voice said, "My name is Julius Graham. I got your name from my math teacher. She said you're a tutor, and I was wondering if you had any openings to tutor me."

"What class are you in?" Denim asked casually as she linked her arm with her fathers.

"I'm in honors algebra. She said you were one of the best."

Denim smiled and said, "Thank you. I can't give you a definite answer right now, but let me check my appointment book and I'll call you back."

"Sounds good," Julius replied before hanging up.

As Julius made his way into the store for his mother, he hoped that the tutor could help him get his grade back up where it needed to be. It wasn't that he was a bad student. In fact, his grades had been A's and B's, until he started getting distracted by his mother's illness, his dad's job loss, and the ever-growing crime in the neighborhood.

Just when the family had found a better neighborhood to move into, his father was laid off from his job of fifteen years, putting a halt on all their plans. He knew at that point he would have to step up and do what he had to do to help his family. Julius came from a family with a long history of hardworking men of strong faith. His prayer was for the obstacles weighing down on his family to be resolved so they could get back to a normal life, and Denim Mitchell just might be the positive link he needed to seek his salvation.